REVISED AND UP
SECOND EDITION

EVERYONE LIKES TO EAT

How Children Can Eat Most of the Foods They Enjoy and Still Take Care of Their Diabetes

HUGO J. HOLLERORTH, ED.D.,
AND DEBRA KAPLAN, R.D., M.S.

with Anna Maria Bertorelli, M.B.A., R.D., C.D.E.

written in conjunction with the Joslin Diabetes Center

CHRONIMED PUBLISHING

Everyone Likes to Eat: How children can eat most of the foods they enjoy and still take care of their diabetes. © 1993 by Joslin Diabetes Center

All rights reserved. Except for brief passages for review purposes, no part of this publication may be reproduced, stored in a retrieval system or transmitted, in any form or by any means, electronic, photocopying, recording, or otherwise, without the prior written permission of CHRONIMED Publishing.

Library of Congress Cataloging-in-Publication Data

Hollerorth, Hugo J., Ed.D.

Everyone Likes to Eat: How children can eat most of the foods they enjoy and still take care of their diabetes / Hugo J. Hollerorth

    p.   cm.

Debra Kaplan, R.D., M.S., with Anna Maria Bertorelli, M.B.A., R.D., C.D.E.

ISBN 1-5656-026-1

1. Diabetes in children-Diet therapy-Juvenile literature.
(1. Diabetes. 2. Diabetics-Nutrition.)

RJ420.D5H65 1993	93-1534
618.92'4620654–dc20	CIP
	AC

Edited by: Richard Graber
Cover and Text Design and Production: MacLean and Tuminelly
Cover and Text Illustrations: Caroline Price
Production Manager: Claire Lewis

Printed in the United States of America

Published by CHRONIMED Publishing
P.O. Box 47945
Minneapolis, MN 55447-9727

TABLE OF CONTENTS

WHAT YOU NEED TO KNOW ABOUT DIABETES..............2
Check these basic terms..............2
What does this have to do with diabetes?..............3
With diabetes, your pancreas does not make insulin..............4

TAKING INSULIN SHOTS..............5
Two kinds of insulin..............5
The daily shots..............9
How the shots work with your meals..............9
How much insulin..............10

FOLLOWING A MEAL PLAN..............13
Food groups..............13
On to your meal plan..............17
Food choices and limits..............19
Meal plan timing..............21
Miscellaneous foods..............23
Figuring pizza..............25

HELPFUL AND HEALTHFUL CHOICES..............33
Fiber..............33
Fat..............36

Sugar 39
Snacks 41
Make your own snacks 46
Breakfast 48
Meat choices 50
School lunches 51
Fast food restaurants 56

EXERCISE 61

Extra snacks 62
Your exercise pattern 64

BIRTHDAY PARTIES, HALLOWEEN, AND OTHER STUFF 67

Birthday parties 68
Your own birthday party 68
A friend's birthday party 70
Halloween 71
School parties 73
Slumber parties 75
Camping trips 76
Thanksgiving and other holidays 78

FOOD LISTS 81

FAST FOOD RESTAURANTS 114

EVERYONE LIKES TO EAT

We all like to eat good food. Kids, moms, dads, grandpas and grandmas, friends. Who doesn't like the smell of vegetable soup bubbling on the stove, the aroma of a special cake right out of the oven, the taste of roast chicken and dressing?

And a hamburger tastes great, especially when you are out eating it with friends.

Good food not only tastes great, it's necessary, of course, for building strong muscles and bones, for giving us energy for everything we do. Even asleep, we use up energy.

Okay, so you have diabetes. Don't think for a minute that you are going to have to give up everything you like to eat.

Sure, some foods are definitely out most of the time when you have diabetes—things like candy bars, cake frosting, hot fudge sundaes. Still, you have many choices, and this book helps you find out what they are.

How about pizza?... Sure! Hamburgers?... Of course. Spaghetti?... Why not?

And you'll be able to go to birthday parties and sleep-overs. Or go trick-or-treating on Halloween. You'll be able to enjoy school parties and family holiday meals like Thanksgiving. You'll even be able to go on overnight camping trips.

This book tells you what you need to know about the food you eat, so you can take care of your diabetes *and* still enjoy your food. And it's not difficult. Just read a chapter or so every day, then go back whenever you have new foods to think about. And if you need more information, ask your parents, your dietitian, or your doctor. Enjoy!

WHAT YOU NEED TO KNOW ABOUT DIABETES

Before learning how you can eat most of the foods you enjoy and still take care of your diabetes, you need to remember some things about diabetes.

You need to know what parts of your body are affected, what these parts do, and how diabetes affects what these parts do.

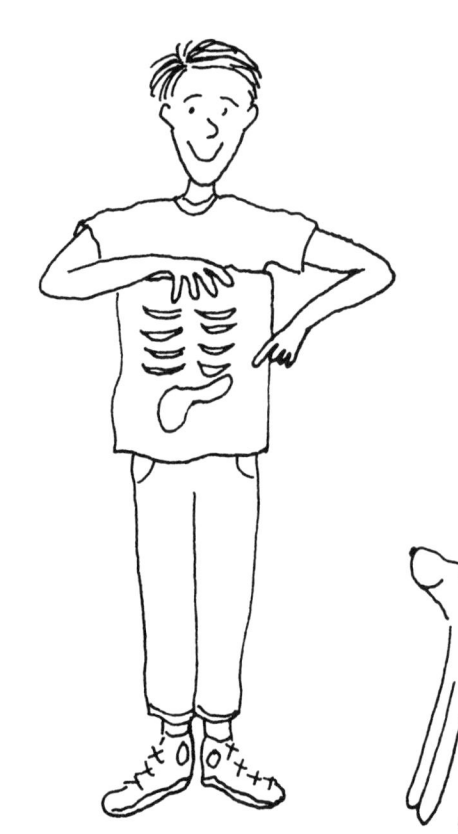

Check these basic terms. (You probably already know them):

- What's the gland just behind the lower part of your stomach that's involved in diabetes?

The **pancreas** (pan-kree-us)

It's the one described as pear-shaped, whale-shaped, or tadpole-shaped.

■ And what does it do?

It makes **insulin,** a hormone very important in diabetes. More on insulin later.

■ Your body is made up of millions of microscopic **body cells**. Are they important in diabetes?

They sure are.

What does this have to do with diabetes?

The **pancreas, insulin,** and **body cells** have a lot to do with diabetes.

Your body changes most of the food you eat into sugar. Your blood carries the sugar to millions and millions of body cells. And the cells use the sugar for energy.

But the body cells can't use sugar for energy without the help of insulin. So the blood carries the insulin made by the pancreas to the body cells. Insulin helps the sugar get inside the body cells so they can use it for energy.

With diabetes, your pancreas does not make insulin. When your pancreas doesn't make insulin, the sugar in your blood can't enter the body cells so they can use it for energy. That's why you may have felt tired all the time just before you found out you have diabetes—sugar from the food you ate wasn't being used for energy.

When sugar can't enter the body cells, a lot of it stays in your blood. Lots of sugar in the blood = high blood sugar, also called **hyperglycemia** (hy-per-gly-SEE-mee-ah).

WHAT YOU NEED TO KNOW ABOUT DIABETES

With diabetes, your pancreas does not make insulin

When your pancreas doesn't produce enough insulin to help your body cells use sugar for energy, you have to do something fast to avoid getting very sick! You probably know this. Before you knew you had diabetes, you probably were very sick—it usually works that way. Maybe your Mom or Dad didn't know what was wrong either until they took you to your doctor. That's when you found out your blood sugar was high (hyperglycemia). It was high because you have diabetes. Sound familiar?

When you know you have diabetes there are some things you to have to do take care of it:

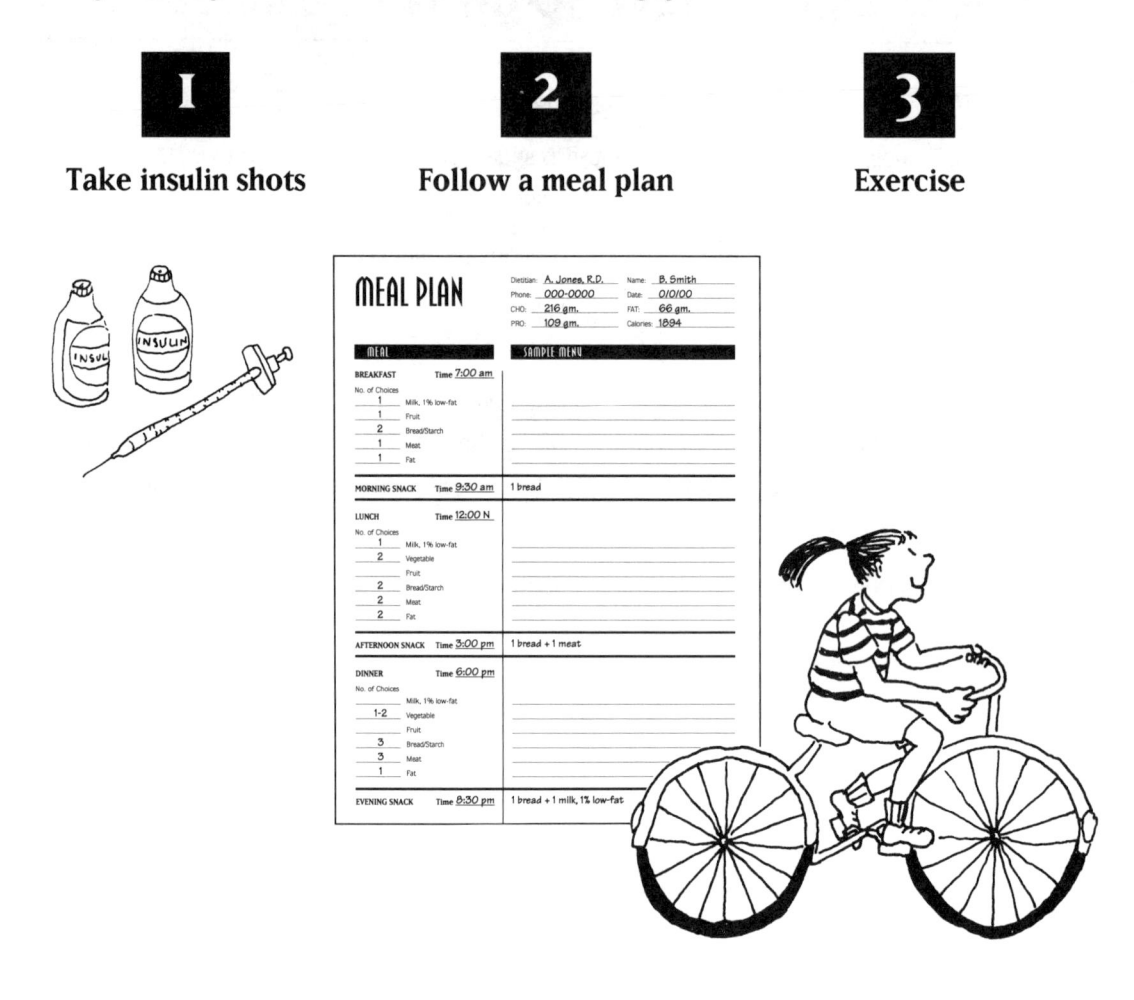

1 Take insulin shots

2 Follow a meal plan

3 Exercise

These are the keys to help you take good care of your diabetes, so you can eat most of the foods you like. First, about those insulin shots....

TAKING YOUR INSULIN SHOTS

Why take insulin shots? Because with diabetes, your pancreas doesn't make insulin. The sugar in your blood can't get into the body cells so they can use it for energy. So, you have to take insulin shots to provide your body with the insulin your pancreas does not make.

Two kinds of insulin

There are two types of insulin most young people with diabetes take: clear and cloudy.

Clear insulin works fast and is called **fast-acting insulin**. How fast does it work? Check the correct answer:

1. Clear insulin starts to work in:

    ____2 hours

    ____1/2 hour

    ____3 hours

When does clear insulin work the hardest?

2. Clear insulin works hardest in:

    ____2 to 4 hours

    ____10 hours

    ____5 hours

TAKING YOUR INSULIN SHOTS

How long does clear insulin work?

3. Clear insulin stops working after:

　　＿＿＿6 to 8 hours

　　＿＿＿1 to 2 hours

　　＿＿＿24 hours

The answers are at the bottom of the page.

ACTION PATTERN OF FAST ACTING INSULIN

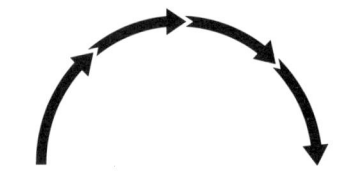

7 am	1 pm	7 pm	1 am	7 am
Breakfast	Lunch	Dinner	Sleep	Breakfast

Answers:
1. 1/2 hour.
2. 2 to 4 hours.
3. 6 to 8 hours.

TAKING YOUR INSULIN SHOTS

Cloudy insulin works slowly and is called the **slow-acting insulin**.

How slow does it work?

1. Cloudy insulin starts to work in:

    _____1/2 hour

    _____12 hours

    _____1 to 3 hours

When does cloudy insulin work the hardest?

2. Cloudy insulin works hardest in:

    _____2 to 3 hours

    _____6 to 12 hours

    _____6 to 8 hours

How long does it work?

3. Cloudy insulin stops working after:

    _____18 to 26 hours

    _____12 hours

    _____1 hour

See the answers at the bottom of the page.

Answers:
1. 1 to 3 hours.
2. 6 to 12 hours.
3. 18 to 26 hours.

TAKING YOUR INSULIN SHOTS

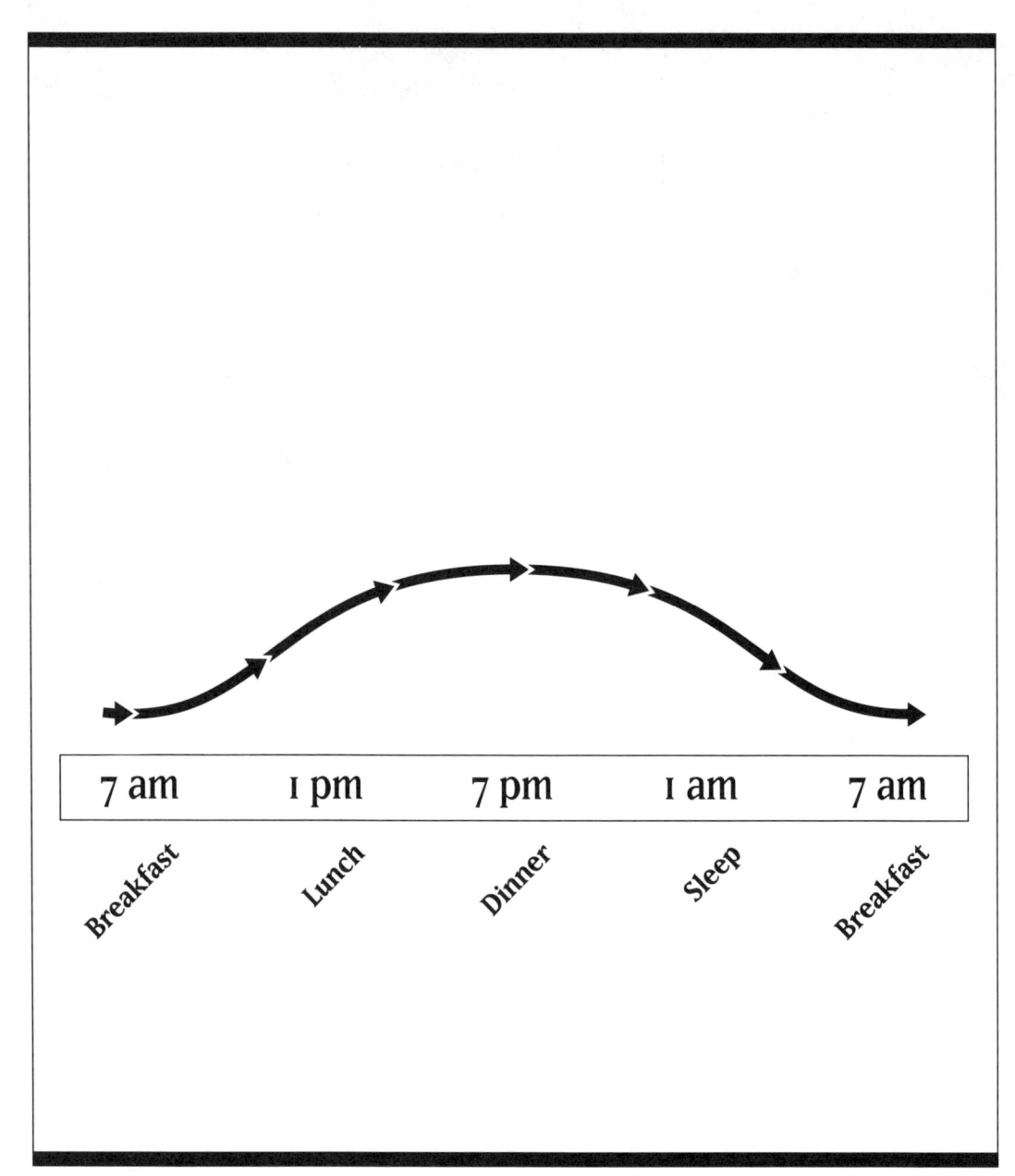

ACTION PATTERN OF SLOW-ACTING INSULIN

| 7 am | 1 pm | 7 pm | 1 am | 7 am |

Breakfast   Lunch   Dinner   Sleep   Breakfast

TAKING YOUR INSULIN SHOTS

The daily shots

Many of you with diabetes take two insulin shots every day, one shot about 1/2 hour before breakfast, and usually another shot about 1/2 hour before dinner. Most often each shot is a mixture of clear insulin and cloudy insulin.

How the shots work with your meals

The drawing on this page shows how the different insulins work when you eat your meals.

Clear insulin in the morning shot starts to work fast. It helps sugar from the food you eat for breakfast get into the body cells. But it loses its effect around noon. To make up for this, the cloudy insulin in the morning shot is working hard by noon. It helps the sugar from the food you eat for lunch get into the body cells.

Clear, fast-acting insulin before dinner helps sugar from the food you eat get into the body cells, the way it did before breakfast. The cloudy insulin before dinner helps your body use sugar in the blood for energy while you are sleeping. And your body does need energy even when you are sleeping.

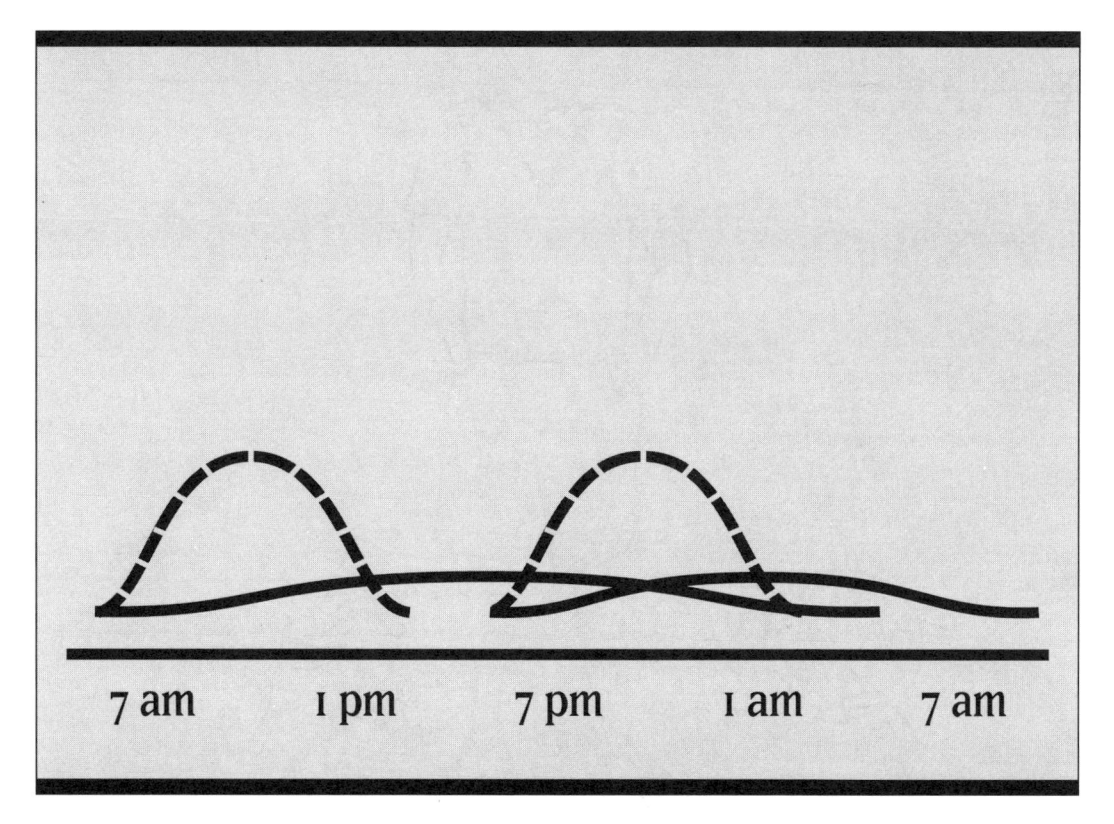

- - - = FAST-ACTING INSULIN

——— = SLOW-ACTING INSULIN

(Graph showing insulin activity from 7 am, 1 pm, 7 pm, 1 am, 7 am)

TAKING YOUR INSULIN SHOTS

How much insulin?

Your doctor will prescribe how much clear and cloudy insulin you should use. The amount will help your body cells use the sugar from the food you eat for energy. And, it will also help keep the amount of sugar in your blood from getting too high, the way it probably was when you first found out you had diabetes.

Milligrams and deciliters are used to measure the amount of sugar in blood—just like pints and quarts are used to measure milk. Your doctor will tell you a high number and a low number for blood sugar levels. The numbers might be 140 and 70. Or they could be 180 and 80. They could be other numbers, too. Try to keep your blood sugar between the numbers your doctor tells you.

That's everything you need to know about insulin, at least for now.

Got it all straight so far? Check yourself by doing the word scramble on page 11. Connect each word with the sentence that describes it. (Then cover yours and have your parents do theirs. Everyone needs reminders.)

TAKING YOUR INSULIN SHOTS

WORD SCRAMBLE TO REVIEW SO FAR

Draw a line from each word in Column 1 to the sentence in Column 2 that best describes it. The correct answers are printed upside down at the bottom of the page.

Column 1

1. Clear

2. Clear insulin in the morning shot

3. Same time every day

4. Two

5. In 6 to 12 hours

6. After 1/2 hour

7. Cloudy insulin in shot before dinner

Column 2

A. When insulin should be taken.

B. A kind of insulin used by boys and girls with diabetes.

C. When cloudy insulin works the hardest.

D. Helps sugar from the food you eat for breakfast get into the body cells.

E. The number of insulin shots most boys and girls take every day.

F. Helps your body use sugar in the blood for energy while you are sleeping.

G. When clear insulin starts to work.

Answers:
1-B; 2-D; 3-A; 4-E; 5-C; 6-G; 7-F.

TAKING YOUR INSULIN SHOTS

WORD SCRAMBLE FOR YOUR PARENTS

Draw a line from each word in Column 1 to the sentence in Column 2 that best describes it. The correct answers are printed upside down at the bottom of the page.

Column 1

1. Clear

2. Clear insulin in the morning shot

3. Same time every day

4. Two

5. In 6 to 12 hours

6. After 1/2 hour

7. Cloudy insulin in shot before dinner

Column 2

A. When insulin should be taken.

B. A kind of insulin used by boys and girls with diabetes.

C. When cloudy insulin works the hardest.

D. Helps sugar from the food you eat for breakfast get into the body cells.

E. The number of insulin shots most boys and girls take every day.

F. Helps your body use sugar in the blood for energy while you are sleeping.

G. When clear insulin starts to work.

Answers:
1-B; 2-D; 3-A; 4-E; 5-C; 6-G; 7-F.

FOLLOWING A MEAL PLAN

In addition to insulin shots, the second thing you have to do if you want to eat most of the foods you enjoy and also take care of your diabetes is to follow a meal plan.

A meal plan tells you how many choices of food you can have at each meal from each of the food groups. Since you can't follow a meal plan unless you know about food groups, let's review them first.

Food groups

All foods are divided into six food groups——**meat, vegetables, fruit, bread, milk, fat.**

Check the drawings of four foods. Which of the four is different from the other three?

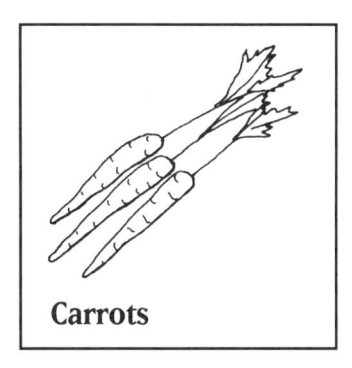

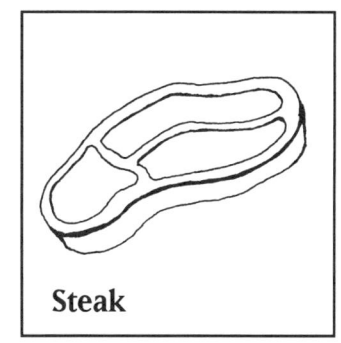

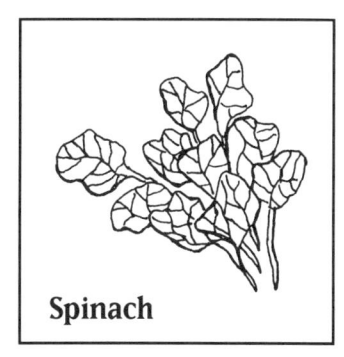

| Carrots | Green beans | Steak | Spinach |

Write your answer here: _____

Steak is the right answer. Steak is a **meat**, and carrots, green beans, and spinach are **vegetables**. **Meat** and **vegetables** are two of the six groups.

FOLLOWING A MEAL PLAN

Check the four foods pictured. Which of the four is different from the other three?

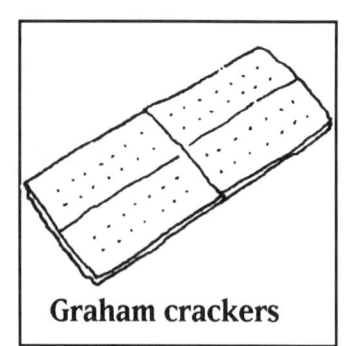

| Bread | Apple | Corn flakes | Graham crackers |

Answer _____

Apple is correct. It's a **fruit**, and bread, corn flakes, and graham crackers are **breads** (sometimes called starches). **Fruit** and **bread/starch** are two more of the six food groups. Two to go.

Finally, check the food pictured below. Which is different from the other three?

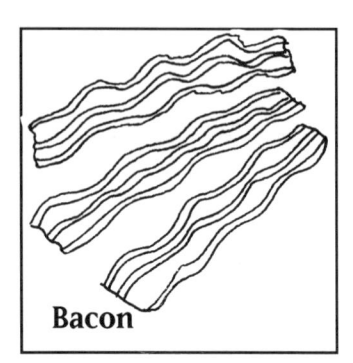

| Bacon | Butter | Milk | Mayonnaise |

Answer _____

Skim milk is correct, although this pick is tougher, right? Skim milk belongs to the **milk** group, which also includes low-fat milk, whole milk, sugar-free cocoa, and yogurt. Bacon, butter, and mayonnaise belong to the **fat** group—foods loaded with fat. Why not include bacon in the meat group? Because it has more fat in it than other meats.

FOLLOWING A MEAL PLAN

Some other foods belong to groups that may seem strange. Corn and peas belong to the **bread/starch** group, not to the vegetable group, because they are loaded with starch. So do potatoes and lima beans.

So, now you know the six food groups. Can you remember all of them?

HERE'S A REMINDER:

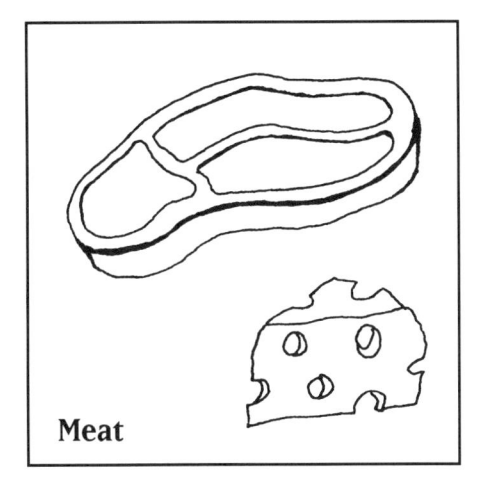

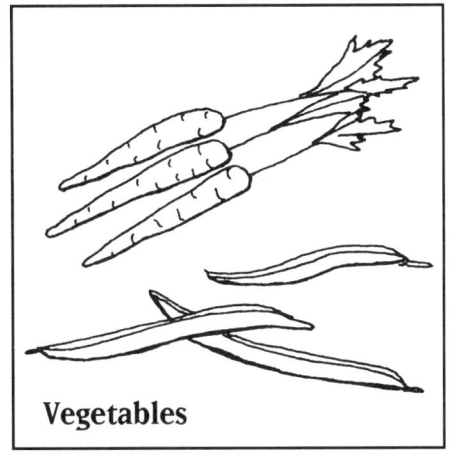

Meat

Vegetables

Fruit

Bread/Starch

Milk

Fat

MEAT LIST

includes beef, pork, fish, poultry, eggs, cheese, and meat substitutes

VEGETABLE LIST

includes fresh, frozen, and canned vegetables

MILK LIST

includes nonfat (skim), low-fat, and whole milk, yogurt, and sugar-free cocoa

FRUIT LIST

includes fresh fruit, pure fruit juice, and canned, dried, cooked, or frozen fruit (without additional sugar)

BREAD/STARCH LIST

includes bread, crackers, cereal, pasta, starchy vegetables, and other selected items

FAT LIST

includes butter, margarine, cream, mayonnaise, nuts, salad dressings, vegetable oils, and other selected items

FOLLOWING A MEAL PLAN

On to your meal plan

A meal plan tells you how many choices of food you may have at each meal from each of the food groups. Your own meal plan, usually made with the help of a dietitian, is special for your needs. No single meal plan is right for everyone.

Page 18 has a meal plan to study. Yours will be different, but let's see how this one works.

Look under Breakfast. If this were your plan, you could have food from the **milk, fruit, bread/starch, meat,** and **fat** food groups. Why no **vegetable** listed? Because vegetables are seldom eaten for breakfast.

Look again under Breakfast. The numbers tell you how many choices of food you may have for breakfast from each of the food groups.

FOLLOWING A MEAL PLAN

MEAL PLAN

Dietitian: **A. Jones, R.D.** Name: **B. Smith**
Phone: **000-0000** Date: **0/0/00**
CHO: **216 gm.** FAT: **66 gm.**
PRO: **109 gm.** Calories: **1894**

MEAL	SAMPLE MENU
BREAKFAST Time **7:00 am**	
No. of Choices	
1 Milk, 1% low-fat	
1 Fruit	
2 Bread/Starch	
1 Meat	
1 Fat	
MORNING SNACK Time **9:30 am**	1 bread
LUNCH Time **12:00 N**	
No. of Choices	
1 Milk, 1% low-fat	
2 Vegetable	
_____ Fruit	
2 Bread/Starch	
2 Meat	
2 Fat	
AFTERNOON SNACK Time **3:00 pm**	1 bread + 1 meat
DINNER Time **6:00 pm**	
No. of Choices	
_____ Milk, 1% low-fat	
1-2 Vegetable	
_____ Fruit	
3 Bread/Starch	
3 Meat	
1 Fat	
EVENING SNACK Time **8:30 pm**	1 bread + 1 milk, 1% low-fat

18

FOLLOWING A MEAL PLAN

Food choices and limits

How do you know what foods are in the **bread/starch** group? Turn to page 90. The list there names all the foods in the **bread/starch** group.

It includes various breads like English muffins and whole wheat bread, lots of cereals, crackers, and other foods. As the sample meal plan on page 18 shows, you could choose any two. You could choose an English muffin and corn flakes, or a bagel and Rice Krispies™. But you couldn't just eat until you are stuffed. You couldn't eat the whole box of Rice Krispies at one time.

The list tells you not only what foods in the **bread/starch** food group you can eat, but also how much. If you choose an English muffin and corn flakes, the **bread/starch** list tells you that you could have 1/2 of an English muffin and 3/4 cup of corn flakes.

If you choose a bagel and Rice Krispies, you could have 1/2 of a bagel and 3/4 cup of Rice Krispies.

If you choose the foods in the list below, using your own meal plan, how much of each food could you have?

AMOUNT	FOOD
_____	Raisin bread
_____	Bulkie roll
_____	All Bran™ with Extra Fiber
_____	Grapenut Flakes™
_____	Shredded Wheat™ (spoon size)
_____	Cooked cereal
_____	Rice cakes
_____	Stella D'Oro Egg Biscuit™

FOLLOWING A MEAL PLAN

Of course, you could use both of your **bread/starch** choices with the same food. You could have two halves of a whole English muffin. You could have two times the 3/4 of a cup of Rice Krispies —1 1/2 cups.

Most of the time, however, it is better to choose more than one kind of food. Different foods contain different vitamins and minerals your body needs.

Why the limits? Why can't you eat all the Rice Krispies you want?

Remember, your body changes most of the food you eat into sugar. And insulin shots help your body cells use the sugar for energy. If you eat too much food, there won't be enough insulin to help your body cells use the sugar. Then too much sugar will stay in your blood. The result: high blood sugar (hyperglycemia), which can make you very sick.

So, when you choose a food from a food list, don't eat more than your meal plan allows.

FOLLOWING A MEAL PLAN

Meal plan timing

Under Breakfast, the word "Time" appears in the square with 7:00 a.m. beside it. If this were your meal plan, it would mean that you should always eat your breakfast about seven o'clock in the morning.

MEAL PLAN

Dietitian: A. Jones, R.D.　　Name: B. Smith
Phone: 000-0000　　Date: 0/0/00
CHO: 216 gm.　　FAT: 66 gm.
PRO: 109 gm.　　Calories: 1894

MEAL	SAMPLE MENU
BREAKFAST　Time 7:00 am No. of Choices 　1　Milk, 1% low-fat 　1　Fruit 　2　Bread/Starch 　1　Meat 　1　Fat	
MORNING SNACK　Time 9:30 am	1 bread
LUNCH　Time 12:00 N No. of Choices 　1　Milk, 1% low-fat 　2　Vegetable 　　　Fruit 　2　Bread/Starch 　2　Meat 　2　Fat	
AFTERNOON SNACK　Time 3:00 pm	1 bread + 1 meat
DINNER　Time 6:00 pm No. of Choices 　　　Milk, 1% low-fat 　1-2　Vegetable 　　　Fruit 　3　Bread/Starch 　3　Meat 　1　Fat	
EVENING SNACK　Time 8:30 pm	1 bread + 1 milk, 1% low-fat

FOLLOWING A MEAL PLAN

Why?

Remember the earlier talk about insulin? Many boys and girls with diabetes have an insulin shot 1/2 hour before breakfast and another 1/2 hour before dinner. And each shot is usually a mixture of clear insulin and cloudy insulin. The clear insulin begins to work in about 1/2 hour.

So, if your meal plan says you should eat breakfast at 7:00 a.m., you probably have your insulin shot at 6:30 a.m. This way you are eating your breakfast when your insulin is starting to work. Then your insulin can help your body cells use the sugar from the food you eat for energy.

REMEMBER

Always have your insulin shots at the same time each day.

Always eat your meals at the same time each day.

This means your insulins will be working and ready to help your body use the sugar from the food you eat for energy.

Miscellaneous foods

So far, you have learned how to use foods that belong to one food group in your meal plan. But what about foods made from more than one food group — combination foods?

Take a plain cheese pizza as an example. What foods are in it? What food groups are they from?

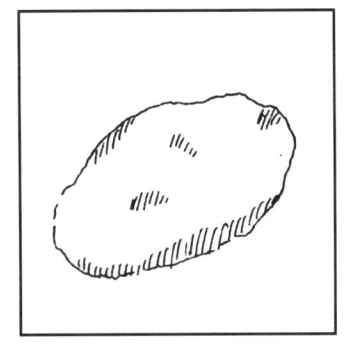

1. First, there is the pizza dough, which is a **bread/starch.**

2. Once the dough is made and placed in a pizza pan, it's brushed with oil. The oil is a **fat.**

3. Then tomato sauce is spread over the oil and dough. Tomato sauce, of course, is a **vegetable**.

4. Finally, the cheese is added. Cheese belongs to the **meat** food group.

So plain cheese pizza is made of foods from four different food groups — **bread/starch, fat, vegetable,** and **meat**. How do you use a combination food like a plain cheese pizza in your meal plan? It's easy because the work has been done for you.

FOLLOWING A MEAL PLAN

Check the miscellaneous food list on page 103. The list has three columns. Combination foods like clam chowder, beef stew, and plain cheese pizza are listed in the first column.

Amounts of each of the foods, such as 8 ounces of clam chowder and 1 cup of beef stew, are listed in the second column.

Listed in the third column are the number **bread/starch, fat, vegetable, meat, milk**, and **fruit** choices the amount equals. For example, 8 ounces of clam chowder equals **1/2 bread/starch, 1 milk** and **1 fat**. One cup of beef stew equals **3 meat, 1 bread/starch**, and **1 vegetable**.

8 Ounces of Clam Chowder
= 1/2 bread/starch
  1 milk
  1 fat

1 Cup of Beef Stew
= 3 meat
  1 bread/starch
  1 vegetable

Figuring pizza

Plain cheese pizza is in the first column in the miscellaneous food list on page 104. The second column says one slice of a 14-inch pizza cut into eight parts equals one portion.

Now, check column 3 to find out the number of **bread/starch**, **fat**, **vegetable**, **meat**, **milk**, and **fruit choices** this amount of pizza equals.

Write the numbers below.

_____ bread/starch

_____ fat

_____ vegetable

_____ meat

_____ milk

_____ fruit

SUBSTITUTION RULES

You may have been taught that you can **substitute** some exchanges for others. Here's how that works.

1 Milk = 1 Bread/Starch + 1 Meat

3 Vegetables = 1 Bread/Starch

1 Vegetable = 1/3 Bread/Starch

1 Fruit = 1 Bread

FOLLOWING A MEAL PLAN

Now look at the lunch part of a meal plan printed on the next page. If this were your meal plan how many choices of **bread/starch**, **meat**, **vegetable**, and **fat** could you have for lunch?

_____ bread/starch

_____ fat

_____ vegetable

_____ meat

_____ milk

_____ fruit

26

MEAL PLAN

Dietitian: **A. Jones, R.D.**
Phone: **000-0000**
CHO: **216 gm.**
PRO: **109 gm.**

Name: **B. Smith**
Date: **0/0/00**
FAT: **66 gm.**
Calories: **1894**

MEAL	SAMPLE MENU

BREAKFAST — Time **7:00 am**

No. of Choices
- 1 — Milk, 1% low-fat
- 1 — Fruit
- 2 — Bread/Starch
- 1 — Meat
- 1 — Fat

MORNING SNACK — Time **9:30 am**

1 bread

LUNCH — Time **12:00 N**

No. of Choices
- 1 — Milk, 1% low-fat
- 2 — Vegetable
- ___ — Fruit
- 2 — Bread/Starch
- 2 — Meat
- 2 — Fat

AFTERNOON SNACK — Time **3:00 pm**

1 bread + 1 meat

DINNER — Time **6:00 pm**

No. of Choices
- ___ — Milk, 1% low-fat
- 1-2 — Vegetable
- ___ — Fruit
- 3 — Bread/Starch
- 3 — Meat
- 1 — Fat

EVENING SNACK — Time **8:30 pm**

1 bread + 1 milk, 1% low-fat

FOLLOWING A MEAL PLAN

FOLLOWING A MEAL PLAN

Now, compare the number of **bread/starch, meat, vegetable**, and **fat** choices that this slice of pizza equals with the number of choices of **bread/starch, meat, vegetable**, and **fat** on the meal plan. How much pizza could you have for lunch?

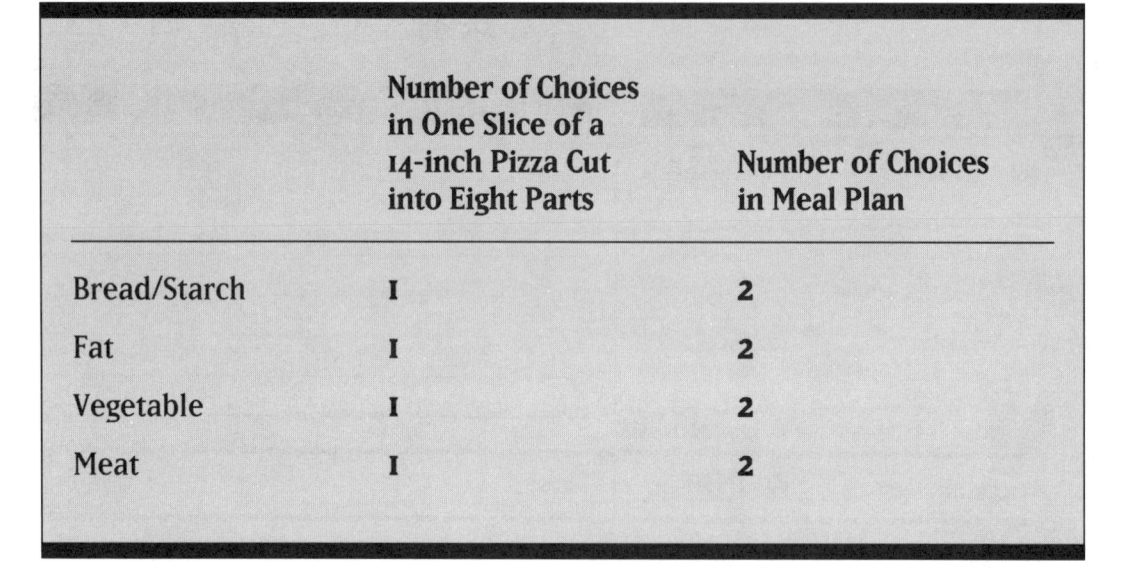

	Number of Choices in One Slice of a 14-inch Pizza Cut into Eight Parts	Number of Choices in Meal Plan
Bread/Starch	1	2
Fat	1	2
Vegetable	1	2
Meat	1	2

The answer:

1 slice of a 14-inch pizza, cut into eight parts equals **1 bread/starch**, **1 fat**, **1 vegetable**, and **1 meat.**

But the meal plan says you can have **2 bread/starch**, **2 fat**, **2 vegetable**, and **2 meat**, so you could have twice as much.

(1/8 + 1/8 = 2/8.)

In other words, you could have two slices of a 14-inch pizza cut into eight pieces for lunch.

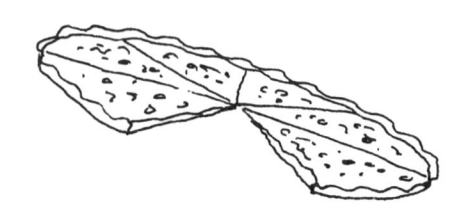

FOLLOWING A MEAL PLAN

Let's imagine that any of the three lunch meal plans on this and the next two pages is one of yours. How would you figure how many slices of plain cheese pizza to eat for lunch?

You now know that one slice of a 14-inch pizza cut into eight equal parts is equal to

1 bread/starch, 1 meat, 1 vegetable, and 1 fat.

1. YOUR LUNCH MEAL PLAN:

1 Milk

1 Vegetable

1 Fruit

2 Bread/Starch

2 Meats

1 Fat

Answer: You could eat 2 slices of plain cheese pizza. That would equal:

2 Bread/Starch, **2 Meats**, **2 Vegetables**, and **2 Fats**.

You would be over 1 vegetable and 1 fat, but that's okay. You could take away one fat from another meal. Getting one or two extra vegetables in your diet in a day is fine.

Be sure to also complete your lunch with 8 ounces (1 cup) of milk and a piece of fruit.

FOLLOWING A MEAL PLAN

2. YOUR LUNCH MEAL PLAN:

1 Vegetable

1 Fruit

3 Bread/Starch

2 Meats

1 Fat

Answer: Again, you could eat 2 slices of plain cheese pizza. Just as in example number 1 above, that equals **2 Bread/Starch, 2 Meats, 2 Vegetables, and 2 Fats**.

You would be over 1 vegetable and 1 fat, but that's okay. Be sure to eat the third bread choice, maybe as crackers, plain cookies, or popcorn. Include a piece of fruit, too.

3. YOUR LUNCH MEAL PLAN:

1 Milk

1 Fruit

3 Bread/Starch

2 Meats

1 Fat

Use the substitution rule we mentioned earlier.

1 Bread/Starch = 3 Vegetables

Then you could have 2 slices of pizza or what's equal to:

2 Bread/Starch, 2 Meats, 2 Vegetables, 2 Fats.

You would be short 1 vegetable (or 1/3 bread), but that's okay. You could also take away one fat from another meal. Be sure to have 8 ounces (1 cup) of milk and a piece of fruit to complete your lunch.

HELPFUL AND HEALTHFUL CHOICES

You can eat most of the foods you enjoy and still take care of your diabetes. However, some food is extra helpful in caring for diabetes, while other food can cause trouble if you eat too much of it.

Fiber

Foods with fiber in them are extra good for you. You'll find fiber in the skin of fresh fruit like apples, in fresh vegetables, in dried beans and peas, in nuts, seeds, and popcorn.

Foods made with bran like whole wheat bread, bran muffins, and bran cereals, are high in fiber. Foods made from oat bran like oat meal, oat bran cereals, and oat bran muffins are excellent for you.

Why fiber?

When you eat foods with lots of fiber in them, your blood sugar may rise more slowly after eating. This means your insulin has more time to help your body cells use the sugar in your blood for energy. Then there is less chance of having high blood sugar.

Find out what foods are high in fiber and use them whenever possible. Try the quick test on the next page. Which foods are high in fiber? Look at the answers on the bottom of the page to see if you chose the right foods.

HELPFUL AND
HEALTHFUL CHOICES

QUIZ: WHICH HAS MORE FIBER?

1. ORANGE JUICE **OR** A WHOLE, FRESH ORANGE
2. APPLESAUCE **OR** A WHOLE, FRESH APPLE
3. BAKED POTATO WITH SKIN **OR** MASHED POTATO
4. COOKED CARROTS **OR** RAW CARROTS
5. POPCORN **OR** POTATO CHIPS
6. ENGLISH MUFFIN **OR** OAT BRAN MUFFIN

Answers:

1. A whole fresh orange is better than orange juice. Orange slices have lots of fiber.
2. A whole fresh apple is the best. There is lots of fiber in the skin of a fresh apple.
3. Choose the baked potato and eat the skin as well as the inside part. The skin on a baked potato will add lots of fiber to your meal.
4. The raw carrot is the best choice. Raw vegetables are a good source of fiber.
5. Popcorn is the best choice. Popcorn has lots of fiber. Pop your popcorn with a hot-air popcorn popper, and you won't have to use lots of fat (butter). You can eat a lot, too. Three cups of popped popcorn equals 1 bread/starch.
6. Bran and corn muffins have more fiber than most other muffins. Oat bran muffins are best of all. Want to make some? The recipe is on page 35. Ask a growup for help.

Banana Oat Bran Muffins

1 muffin = 1 bread/starch + 1 fat

2 tablespoons margarine, melted

2 tablespoons sugar

1/4 cup low-cholesterol egg substitute or 1 egg

1/4 cup buttermilk

1/2 cup unprocessed bran

1/2 cup whole wheat flour

1/2 teaspoon baking soda

1/2 teaspoon salt (optional)

1 teaspoon baking powder

1/2 cup oat bran

1 cup chopped bananas (1 medium banana)

Mix margarine and sugar. Add egg substitute, buttermilk, and unprocessed bran. Allow to stand while preparing other ingredients. In another bowl, sift together the flour, baking soda, salt and baking powder. Add this to the first mixture. Add the oat bran and chopped banana. Mix just until ingredients are combined. Bake in muffin tins sprayed with a non-stick spray at 400 degrees for 20 to 25 minutes. Makes 12 muffins.

Fat

When drain pipes get clogged up, water has a hard time flowing. When gutters get clogged up, rain water can't flow through. When noses get clogged, people have a hard time breathing. In the same way, the blood vessels which carry blood to all parts of our bodies can become clogged up. Then the blood has a hard time carrying sugar from the food you eat to the millions and millions of cells in your body where it is used for energy.

What clogs the blood vessels?

The fat in some kinds of food clog the blood vessels if we eat too much of it. Most of the kind of fat that clogs is in food that comes from animals.

It's in red meat like beef and pork and lamb.

It's also in eggs, whole milk, and foods made from whole milk like butter and cheese.

There is also lots of fat in the skin of chicken and turkey.

The fat in all of these foods collects in the blood vessels and slows down the flow of blood to the cells of the body.

It's better to eat chicken and turkey without the skin. There's still some fat, but not as much as in red meat like beef and pork. Also, fish and 1% low-fat or skim milk, cheese made from skim milk, and substitutes for eggs are low in fat.

Fat is found in some vegetables like corn and soybeans and safflower, sunflower, and cotton seeds. Margarine, which can be used in place of butter, is made from oils in these foods. So are some of the oils used in cooking.

These vegetable fats don't clog your blood vessels.

Ask your parents to use soft, tub margarine instead of butter and to use oils from vegetables and seeds for cooking instead of butter, lard, and shortening. (Liquid fats are better for you than solid fats.)

Try this quick test to be sure you know which foods have less fat in them. Check the next page for answers.

QUIZ: WHICH HAS LESS FAT?

1. WHOLE MILK — OR — 1% LOW-FAT MILK OR 99% FAT-FREE MILK
2. BUTTER — OR — MARGARINE IN TUBS
3. PEANUT BUTTER — OR — BOLOGNA
4. BROILED CHICKEN WITH SKIN REMOVED — OR — FRIED CHICKEN

HELPFUL AND
HEALTHFUL CHOICES

Answers:

1. 1% low-fat or 99% fat-free milk is the best choice. It does not have as much fat as whole milk.

2. Margarine is better than butter. It is made from vegetable fat. Use a soft margarine sold in a small tub.

3. Peanut butter is the best choice. It is made from the fat in nuts, which is better for you than the fat in bologna.

4. Broiled chicken without the skin is better for you than fried chicken. There is lots of fat in the skin. When you broil chicken, the fat drips out into the pan, so there isn't as much fat in the chicken when you eat it. If you remove the skin before eating the chicken, there is even less fat.

38

Sugar

You have diabetes, so a lot of sugar is out. No matter. Some sweetener substitutes work well and are safe for you to use.

Know these words well: aspartame, saccharin, and acesulfame potassium. You may know them better by their other names.

Aspartame is also called Equal®, Nutrasweet®, or Sweet Mate®. Saccharin is also called Sweet 'n Low® or Sweet Magic®. Acesulfame potassium is called Sweet One™ or Swiss Sweet™.

Equal®, Nutrasweet®, Sweet'n Low®, and Swiss Sweet™ are sweeteners. They are added to food to make it taste sweet.

They are like sugar, but they are also different and the difference is very important.

HELPFUL AND HEALTHFUL CHOICES

Sugar makes your blood sugar rise very fast. Sweeteners like "Equal" and "Sweet 'n Low" do not raise your blood sugar.

Because of diabetes, you need to be very careful about eating too much sugar. This can be tricky because different types of sugar have different names. Some of the names to watch out for are:

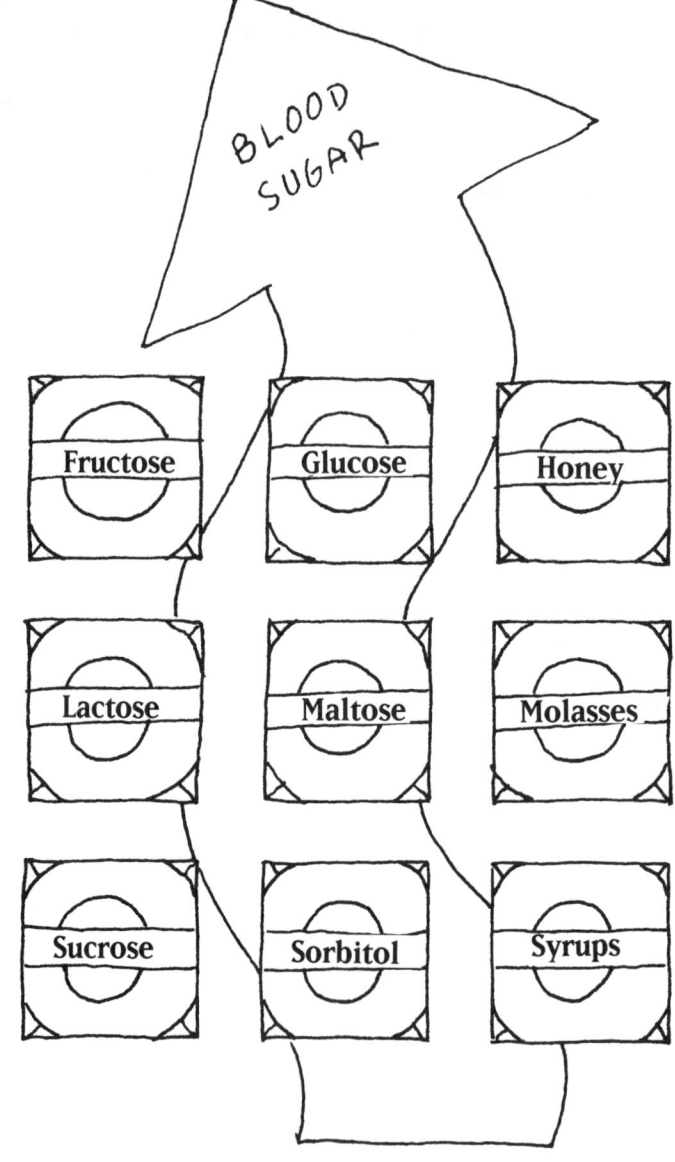

- Fructose
- Glucose
- Honey
- Lactose
- Maltose
- Molasses
- Sucrose
- Sorbitol
- Syrups

It's best not to use these unless your dietitian says you can. Stick with sweeteners like Equal®, Nutrasweet®, Sweet 'n Low®, and Sweet One™.

HELPFUL AND
HEALTHFUL CHOICES

Snacks

Notice the morning snack, afternoon snack, and evening snack in this meal plan. When you take insulin shots, you must eat an afternoon and evening snack. You may also have to eat a morning snack. Why?

MEAL PLAN

Dietitian: A. Jones, R.D.   Name: B. Smith
Phone: 000-0000   Date: 0/0/00
CHO: 216 gm.   FAT: 66 gm.
PRO: 109 gm.   Calories: 1894

MEAL	SAMPLE MENU

BREAKFAST — Time 7:00 am
No. of Choices
- 1 Milk, 1% low-fat
- 1 Fruit
- 2 Bread/Starch
- 1 Meat
- 1 Fat

MORNING SNACK — Time 9:30 am   1 bread

LUNCH — Time 12:00 N
No. of Choices
- 1 Milk, 1% low-fat
- 2 Vegetable
- ___ Fruit
- 2 Bread/Starch
- 2 Meat
- 2 Fat

AFTERNOON SNACK — Time 3:00 pm   1 bread + 1 meat

DINNER — Time 6:00 pm
No. of Choices
- ___ Milk, 1% low-fat
- 1-2 Vegetable
- ___ Fruit
- 3 Bread/Starch
- 3 Meat
- 1 Fat

EVENING SNACK — Time 8:30 pm   1 bread + 1 milk, 1% low-fat

41

HELPFUL AND HEALTHFUL CHOICES

This drawing shows how your insulins work. It's the same drawing you looked at before on page 9. Notice how the insulins work after you have eaten your meals. They help your body use the sugar from the foods you have eaten for energy.

But notice, also, how the insulins keep working long after you have finished eating.

They work all day and even during the night, helping your body use the sugar in your blood for energy.

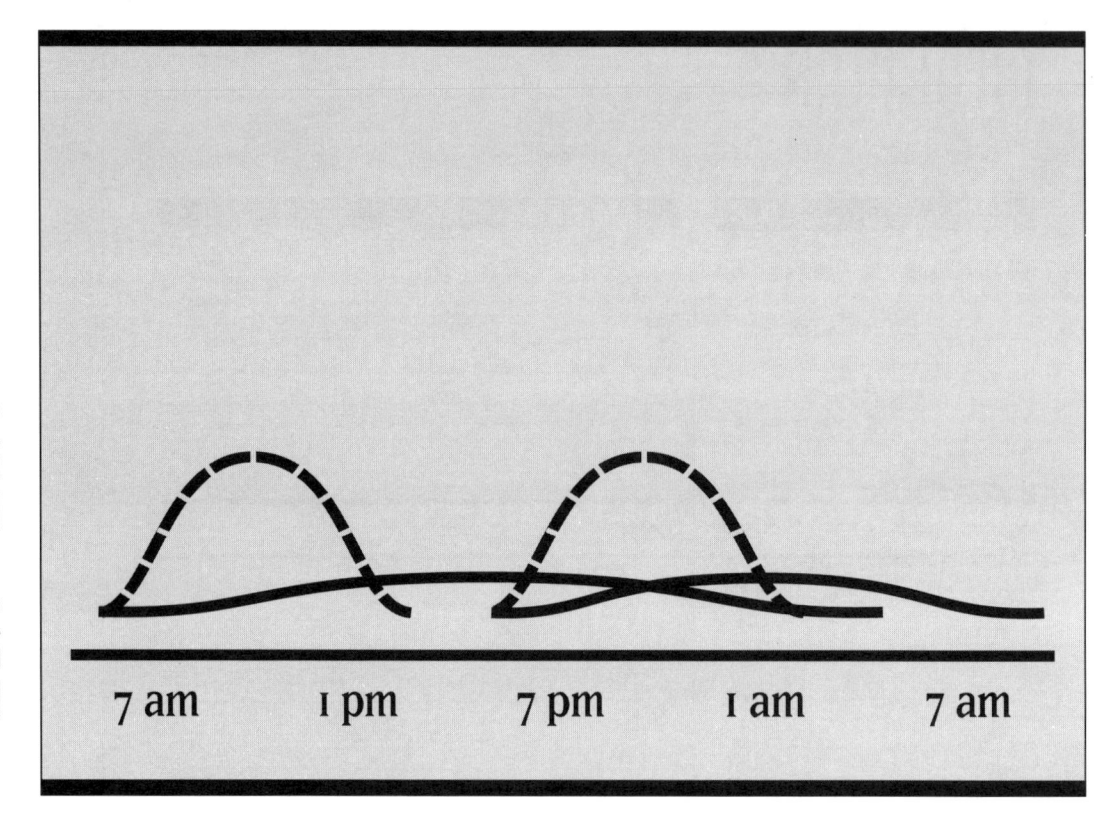

- - - = FAST-ACTING INSULIN

—— = SLOW-ACTING INSULIN

7 am   1 pm   7 pm   1 am   7 am

HELPFUL AND HEALTHFUL CHOICES

By the middle of the afternoon or at bedtime the amount of sugar in your blood may become low.

You could have what is called low blood sugar or hypoglycemia. You might begin to feel shaky, dizzy, weak, tired, cranky, or hungry. You may have a headache. You may feel all or only some of these things.

When you begin to feel this way you may be having an insulin reaction. That's why you need an afternoon and an evening snack if you take insulin shots.

The snack provides more sugar for the body to use for energy and helps to keep you from having low blood sugar. You may need a morning snack, too. Your dietitian will let you know.

What foods should you eat for a snack? The drawing on this page shows four of the six food groups. Arrows between food groups mean you can make a snack by using a food from each of the two food groups.

Snacks

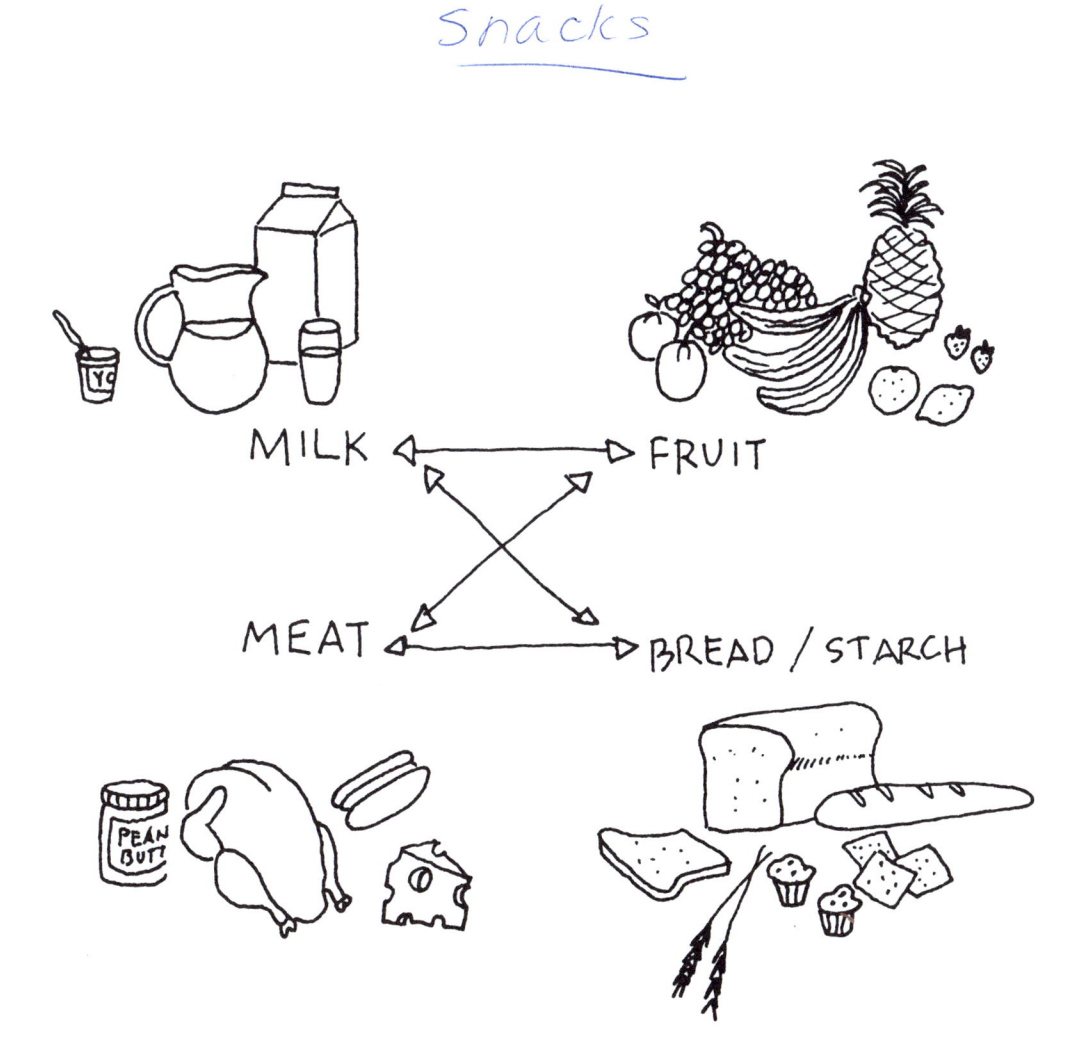

MILK ↔ FRUIT

MEAT ↔ BREAD / STARCH

HELPFUL AND HEALTHFUL CHOICES

Of course you have to use the right amount of each food. See the foods lists on pages 83–107 for the correct amounts.

Check the drawing. Can you use a food from the **milk** food group with a food from the **fruit** food group for a snack?

How about a food from the **milk** food group and one from the **bread/starch** food group?

That's right. It's yes to both questions.

Now for some practice. In the list on the next page, the first snack is crackers and milk. Is this a good snack? Yes, because crackers are a **bread/starch**, milk is a **milk**, and the two groups are connected in the drawing on page 43.

Look at the second snack. What food groups do the foods belong to? If you aren't sure, look at the food lists on pages 83–107.

Can you use foods from these food groups to make a snack? Yes, because turkey is a **meat** and a roll is a **bread** and they are connected.

Do the same for all the other snacks. The correct answers are upside-down below the list of snacks.

HELPFUL AND HEALTHFUL CHOICES

ARE THESE GOOD SNACKS?

1 CRACKERS AND MILK

2 TURKEY AND ROLL

3 CHEESE AND MILK

4 CRACKERS AND PEANUT BUTTER

5 CHEESE AND CRACKERS

6 APPLE AND CRACKERS

7 POPCORN AND PEANUT BUTTER

8 YOGURT AND A BANANA

9 STRAWBERRIES AND MILK

10 YOGURT AND PEANUT BUTTER

Answers:
1. Yes, 2. Yes, 3. No,
4. Yes, 5. Yes, 6. No,
7. Yes, 8. Yes, 9. Yes,
10. No.

HELPFUL AND HEALTHFUL CHOICES

Make your own snacks

You are now ready to make your own snacks. Look at the list of good snacks. The first snack uses a food from the **bread/starch** group with a food from the **milk** group.

SOMETHING TO REMEMBER!

When you use a fruit for a snack, DO NOT USE FRUIT JUICE.

Fruit juice will make your blood sugar rise quickly.

A whole apple is better than apple juice.

A whole orange is better than orange juice.

GOOD SNACKS

	Food Group	Food	Amount
1.	BREAD/STARCH	Cheerios	1 cup
	+		
	MILK	Low-fat milk	1 cup
2.	BREAD/STARCH		
	+		
	MEAT		
3.	FRUIT		
	+		
	MILK		
4.	FRUIT		
	+		
	MEAT		

HELPFUL AND HEALTHFUL CHOICES

How did we choose the foods? We looked at the foods on the "bread/starch list" on page 90 and we chose Cheerios. The list says the right amount to use is one cup.

Then we looked at the "**milk** list" on page 83 and chose a low-fat milk (1%). The correct amount to use is one cup.

Use the food lists on pages 81–107 to make other snacks. This is your chance to eat some of the foods you and your friends see in the stores that look and taste so good.

For a snack that uses a food from the **bread/starch** group, you can choose muffins, popcorn, biscuits. Be careful, though. Some of these foods are made up of more than one food group.

Some crackers, for example, are **1 bread/starch + 1 fat.** So, before using these foods for snacks, look at your meal plan to see if you can have the extra fat choice.

HELPFUL AND HEALTHFUL CHOICES

Breakfast

Every meal is important, but breakfast is most important.

After not eating all night, you may have low blood sugar. Yet you need food for energy so you can get up and go and begin your day. Breakfast helps you play harder, think clearer, and feel better.

The breakfast part of the meal plan on the next page lists one **meat** choice for breakfast. It is very important to eat a food on the **meat** list for breakfast.

Foods on the **meat** list will help keep the right amount of sugar in your blood during the long time between breakfast and lunch. Then you won't run out of energy during that hard arithmetic test just before your lunch hour at school.

MEAL PLAN

Dietitian: __A. Jones, R.D.__ Name: __B. Smith__
Phone: __000-0000__ Date: __0/0/00__
CHO: __216 gm.__ FAT: __66 gm.__
PRO: __109 gm.__ Calories: __1894__

MEAL | SAMPLE MENU

BREAKFAST Time __7:00 am__

No. of Choices
- __1__   Milk, 1% low-fat
- __1__   Fruit
- __2__   Bread/Starch
- __1__   Meat
- __1__   Fat

MORNING SNACK Time __9:30 am__   1 bread

LUNCH Time __12:00 N__

No. of Choices
- __1__   Milk, 1% low-fat
- __2__   Vegetable
- ____   Fruit
- __2__   Bread/Starch
- __2__   Meat
- __2__   Fat

AFTERNOON SNACK Time __3:00 pm__   1 bread + 1 meat

DINNER Time __6:00 pm__

No. of Choices
- ____   Milk, 1% low-fat
- __1-2__   Vegetable
- ____   Fruit
- __3__   Bread/Starch
- __3__   Meat
- __1__   Fat

EVENING SNACK Time __8:30 pm__   1 bread + 1 milk, 1% low-fat

HELPFUL AND HEALTHFUL CHOICES

Meat choices

What can you use for a **meat** choice for breakfast?

Eggs are one possible choice, but you should not eat more than three or four eggs in a week.

Remember, eggs have a kind of fat in them that clogs up the blood vessels. So, go easy on the eggs.

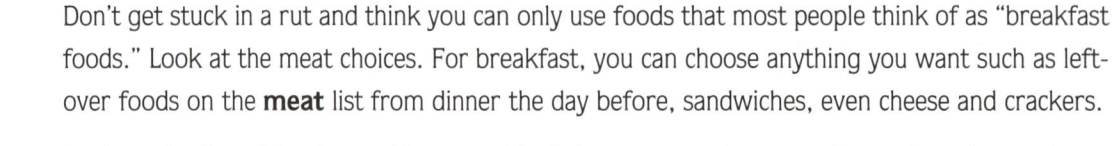

Don't get stuck in a rut and think you can only use foods that most people think of as "breakfast foods." Look at the meat choices. For breakfast, you can choose anything you want such as leftover foods on the **meat** list from dinner the day before, sandwiches, even cheese and crackers.

Look at the list of foods on this page. All of them are on the **meat** list and can be used as a meat choice for breakfast. You and your parents will think of others.

MEAT CHOICES FOR BREAKFAST

(Most foods listed are 1 **meat** choice)

1/2 cup EggBeaters®

1/4 cup low-fat cottage cheese

1 ounce part-skim mozzarella cheese

1 ounce Laughing Cow™ reduced-calorie cheese

1/4 cup (1 ounce) nuts (1 meat + 2 fat)

1/4 cup sunflower seeds (1 meat + 1 fat)

1/4 cup wheat germ (sprinkle wheat germ on cereal)
    (1 low fat meat + 1 bread/starch)

1 tablespoon peanut butter (1 meat + 1 fat)

1 ounce Canadian bacon or lean ham

1/4 cup tuna fish, packed in water

1 ounce sliced turkey or 1 ounce lean roast beef

1 ounce 95 to 98% fat-free cold cuts

HELPFUL AND HEALTHFUL CHOICES

School lunches

If you take a sandwich to school for lunch every day and it's getting a little boring, the following ideas may be just what you need. You can easily change that old boring sandwich into something new and different.

On the next page are four lists. The "outside" list shows some of the many kinds of breads you can use for the outside of your sandwich.

The "inside" list shows some of the meats you can put inside your sandwich. The "on the side" and "endings" lists make suggestions for ways to round out your meal.

Let's use those lists with the chart below to create some favorite lunches.

FAVORITE LUNCH

	Number of choices in my meal plan	Number of choices needed for sandwich	Number of choices needed for On the side and Endings food
Milk			
Vegetable			
Fruit			
Bread/Starch			
Meat			
Fat			

HELPFUL AND
HEALTHFUL CHOICES

CREATING YOUR SANDWICH

OUTSIDE

Whole wheat bread

Rye bread

Pumpernickel bread

Corn or flour tortillas

Syrian (pocket) bread

Bagel

English muffin

Bulkie roll

Frankfurter roll

Matzoh

Rice cakes

Crackers

Cornbread

Bran or corn muffin

ON THE SIDE

Pickles (unsweetened)

Cherry tomatoes

Celery sticks

Cucumber slices

Carrot sticks

Pepper strips

INSIDE

Cheese (lowfat)

Chicken salad

Fish or seafood salad

Tuna salad

Egg salad

Peanut butter and sugar-free jelly

Sliced turkey

Roast beef (lean)

Lean ham

Low-fat cold cuts

Low-fat hotdogs or franks (97% fat-free)

ENDINGS

Fruit (fresh)

Crackers

Muffins

Gingersnaps

Popcorn

Pretzels

Granola bar (plain, raisin, or peanut butter)

HELPFUL AND HEALTHFUL CHOICES

Notice the first column on the chart on page 51. From your own meal plan given to you by your dietitian or doctor, fill in the number of choices you have for lunch from each food group.

Now try to fit a sandwich made from the foods you chose from the outside and inside lists on page 52 into your meal plan.

How many **bread/starch** and **meat** choices do you need for the sandwich? Write the number of choices in the second column. Do you have any **bread/starch** and **meat** choices left over?

Use these along with your **vegetable**, **fruit**, and **fat** choices for the foods you chose from the "On the Side" and "Endings" lists. Can you fit them in? Do you have enough choices? Ask for help if you can't figure it out.

HELPFUL AND
HEALTHFUL CHOICES

On the next page are several examples of school lunches. Look them over and choose the ones you think you would like. Can you fit them into your meal plan? Ask for help if you aren't sure.

If you buy your lunch at school, look in your local newspaper to find out what they are serving, or call the school to find out. And figure out how much of each food you can eat. Ask for help if you need to.

SAMPLE LUNCHES

Milk (1% low-fat)	1 milk
Hamburger roll	2 bread/starch
3-ounce hamburger patty	3 medium-fat meat
Apple	1 fruit

Milk (1% low-fat)	1 milk
2 beef tacos	2 bread/starch, 1 vegetable, 3 medium-fat meat
Orange	1 fruit

Milk (1% low-fat)	1 milk
2 ounces of pita bread	2 bread/starch
1/2 cup of tuna fish	2 lean meat
2 teaspoons of mayonnaise	2 fat
1 pear	1 fruit

Milk (1% low-fat)	1 milk
2 slices pumpernickel bread	2 bread/starch
1/2 cup chicken salad (2 ounces of chicken, 2 teaspoons of mayonnaise)	2 lean meat, 2 fat
3 graham cracker squares	1 bread/starch

Milk (1% low-fat)	1 milk
2 slices whole wheat bread	2 bread/starch
2 tablespoons of peanut butter	2 medium-fat meat + 2 fat
Carrot/celery sticks	1 vegetable
1 banana	2 fruit

HELPFUL AND HEALTHFUL CHOICES

Fast food restaurants

Whether it's Burger King®, McDonald's®, Wendy's®, or some other place, fast food restaurants are favorite places to eat for many boys and girls. However, if you have diabetes, eating in fast food restaurants can be a little tricky because most things served in fast food restaurants are made from foods in the **bread/starch**, **meat**, and **fat** food groups.

So, you have to change the **milk**, **vegetable** and **fruit** choices in your meal plan into **bread/starch**, **meat**, and **fat** choices. Then you have to add them to the **bread**, **meat** and **fat** choices already in your meal plan.

Note:
You shouldn't do this very often, because you won't get the milk, vegetables, and fruit you need to be healthy. It's okay once in a while, however, such as for a party or a special family outing.

How do you change the **milk**, **vegetable**, and **fruit** choices in your meal plan into **bread/starch**, **meat**, and **fat** choices? Suppose, for example, you want to go to McDonald's for a hamburger and French fries.

First you have to remember that:

SUBSTITUTION RULES

1 MILK CHOICE = 1 BREAD/STARCH CHOICE + 1 MEAT CHOICE

3 VEGETABLE CHOICES = 1 BREAD/STARCH CHOICE

1 VEGETABLE CHOICE = 1/3 BREAD/STARCH CHOICE

1 FRUIT CHOICE = 1 BREAD/STARCH CHOICE

HELPFUL AND HEALTHFUL CHOICES

Now look at the lunch part of the meal plan shown below. If this were your meal plan, could you have a hamburger and French fries at McDonald's?

To find out, change the **milk** and **vegetable** choices in the meal plan into **bread/starch**, **meat** and **fat** choices.

Fill in the blanks in the chart below. Then add up the number of **bread/starch**, **meat**, and **fat** choices you can use at McDonald's. Your answer should be 3 2/3 **bread/starches**, 3 **meats** and 2 **fats.**

LUNCH CHOICES IN MEAL PLAN

1 MILK	=	_1_ bread/starch + _1_ meat + ____ fat
2 VEGETABLES	=	_2/3_ bread/starch + ____ meat + ____ fat
2 BREAD/STARCH	=	____ bread/starch + ____ meat + ____ fat
2 MEAT	=	____ bread/starch + ____ meat + ____ fat
2 FAT	=	____ bread/starch + ____ meat + ____ fat
	=	____ bread/starch + ____ meat + ____ fat

HELPFUL AND HEALTHFUL CHOICES

Now find out if you have enough **bread/starch, meat,** and **fat** choices to have a hamburger and French fries at McDonald's.

Look on pages 114–118 for a list of some of the fast food restaurants and some of the foods they serve. The number of **bread/starch, meat,** and **fat** choices they serve is also listed.

Check a McDonald's hamburger. How many **bread/starch, meat,** and **fat** choices are in it? Write the number of choices on the chart.

Do the same for French fries.

Then add up the number of **bread/starch, meat,** and **fat** choices you need for a hamburger and French fries at McDonald's.

Your answer should be **4 bread/starches + 1 1/2 meat + 3 fat**.

If you didn't get the right answer, try again or ask for help.

BREAD/STARCH, MEAT, AND FAT CHOICES IN A McDONALD'S HAMBURGER AND FRENCH FRIES

Hamburger = _____ bread/starch + _____ meat + _____ fat

French fries = _____ bread/starch + _____ meat + _____ fat

_____

Total = _____ bread/starch + _____ meat + _____ fat

HELPFUL AND HEALTHFUL CHOICES

Now compare the number of **bread/starch**, **meat**, and **fat** choices you have from the meal plan on page 57 with the number you need for a hamburger and French fries at McDonald's. The meal plan gives you **3 2/3 bread/starch** choices, and you need **4 bread/starch** choices at McDonald's.

That's close enough.

The meal plan gives you **3 meat** choices, and you need **1 1/2 meat** choices at McDonald's.

That's more than enough. Save the extra **1 1/2 meat** choices and use them in your dinner or evening snack. You can do this with **meat** and **fat** choices for a special outing, but you should never "save" **milk**, **vegetable**, **fruit**, and **bread/starch** choices.

The meal plan gives you two **fat** choices and you need three **fat** choices at McDonald's.

Just this once borrow a **fat** choice from another meal or from a snack.

NUMBER OF BREAD/STARCH, MEAT, AND FAT CHOICES IN MEAL PLAN

3 2/3 bread/starch + 3 meat + 2 fat

NUMBER OF BREAD/STARCH, MEAT, AND FAT CHOICES IN A MCDONALD'S HAMBURGER AND FRENCH FRIES

4 bread/starch + 1 1/2 meat + 3 fat

EXERCISE

You can help care for your diabetes by learning about it, by eating right, and by exercising.

Exercise can mean riding your bike, playing volley ball, swimming, or hiking in the woods.

Exercise makes your muscles, heart, and lungs strong. It helps keep your weight at the right amount. It helps you feel better. And it is fun.

Exercise helps you take care of your diabetes by helping your body cells use insulin more easily.

Extra snacks

Exercise every day and you may not need as much insulin. Also, your muscles use more sugar when you exercise, which helps keep the sugar in your blood from getting too high.

There is one problem, however. Hard exercise like lots of running and jumping can cause low blood sugar (hypoglycemia).

Your muscles use so much sugar for energy that the amount of sugar in your blood gets very low, and you may have an insulin reaction. To prevent this, you may need to eat an extra snack before or during exercise. And if you exercise extra hard, you may also need an extra snack at bedtime.

Whether you need an extra snack when exercising depends on several things —— the kind of exercise, how long you exercise, and whether your blood sugar is high or low before you start.

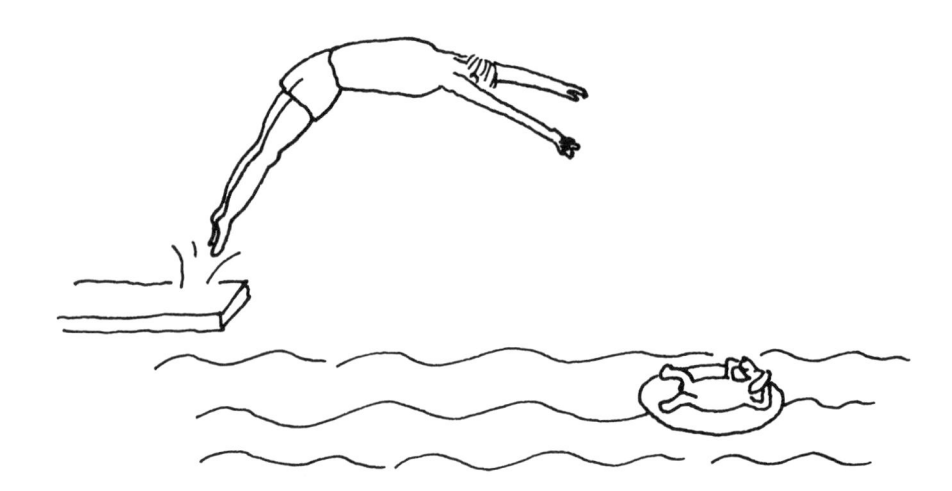

EXERCISE

Keep in mind, your muscles use more sugar for energy when you swim or play basketball than when you walk. Riding your bike for an hour uses more sugar than a quick five-minute bike trip to the home of a friend. And if your blood sugar is already low, you should have an extra snack.

The exercise chart on page 65 will help you decide if you need an extra snack when you exercise and what kind of snack to eat.

If you are going to take a fairly easy bike ride for 30 minutes or less and your blood sugar is between 120 and 180, you may not need an extra snack.

But if you are going to ride your bike for an hour and go a little faster, you may need an extra snack of a bread/starch or fruit. And if you plan to ride for an hour really fast, you may need an extra snack of a bread/starch and a meat.

Your exercise pattern

But be careful.

Exercise lowers the blood sugar of some boys and girls more than it does for others. As you ride your bike or exercise in other ways over a few weeks and months, you'll find out more and more about how exercise lowers your blood sugar.

How? By testing your blood sugar before and after exercising. This will help you decide when you need to eat an extra snack.

EXERCISE AND FOOD

KIND OF EXERCISE	BLOOD SUGAR LEVEL	KIND OF SNACK
1. Fairly easy exercise and less than 30 minutes (such as walking, easy bicycling, baseball, hide and seek, hop scotch, jumping rope).	Less than 70	Treat for low blood sugar
	70-120	1 bread/starch or 1 fruit
	120-240	Do not need extra snack
	*240 or above	Do not need extra snack
2. Somewhat hard exercise for 1 hour (such as swimming, easy bicycling, roller skating, skate boarding, aerobics).	Less than 70	Treat for low blood sugar
	70-120	1 bread/starch + 1 meat
	120-180	1 bread/starch or 1 fruit
	180-240	May not need extra snack
	*240 or above	Do not need extra snack
3. Hard exercise (such as fast bicycling, basketball, hiking, football, soccer and team sports).	Less than 70	Treat for low blood sugar
	70-120	2 bread/starch + 2 meat
	120-180	1 bread/starch + 1 meat
	180-240	1 bread/starch or 1 fruit
	*240 or above	May not need extra snack

*Ask your doctor about extra tests when your blood sugar is 240 or above. You should never exercise when you have ketones in your urine.

EXERCISE

Whether you need an extra snack while exercising depends on several other things also. Remember clear insulin starts to work in 1/2 hour and works hardest in 2 to 4 hours. Cloudy insulin starts to work in 2 to 3 hours and works hardest in 6 to 12 hours.

So, if you exercise when your insulin is working the hardest, you should have an extra snack before you start. This is because hard working insulin and exercise each lower blood sugar. Together they may cause low blood sugar unless you eat an extra snack.

Also, if you are going to exercise a long time, you may need an extra snack while you are doing it. You may even need an extra snack after exercising.

Your doctor may also tell you to decrease the amount of insulin you take on active days. He or she may give you guidelines on how to decrease the amount of insulin that's working hard during the time you exercise.

Your doctor may also tell you where to take your insulin shot. For example, if you're going to play tennis and you use your right arm to swing the racquet, your doctor may tell you to inject into your left arm. Or if you're going to run a race in the afternoon, you may be told to use your arm instead of your leg for your insulin shot. That way, the insulin you take will **not** get into your system too quickly and cause you to have a low blood sugar.

BIRTHDAY PARTIES, HALLOWEEN, AND OTHER STUFF

It's possible to take care of your diabetes and still go to birthday parties and sleep-overs at the homes of your friends. Or go trick-or-treat on Halloween. Or enjoy parties at school and even go on overnight camping trips.

You can do all of these things and more.

BIRTHDAY PARTIES, HALLOWEEN, AND OTHER STUFF

Birthday parties

Having a birthday party or going to the party of a friend? Either way you can have fun.

Yes, you'll have to take it easy with "sweets" like ice cream and cake which are a part of most parties. And that's not easy.

But you can do it and still have fun at the party.

Your own birthday party

Plan your own birthday party around foods you like to eat that also help you take care of your diabetes.

Have your party at lunch or dinner time and invite your friends to a pizza place for pizza or to a fast food restaurant for hamburgers and French fries. After lunch or dinner take your friends swimming or bowling. (The exercise will help you keep your blood sugar down.)

If you go to a pizza place for your party, you already know how to fit plain cheese pizza into your meal plan. (See page 28.) You also know how to find out what foods and how much you can eat at a fast food restaurant.

Remember, you have to change the milk, vegetable, and fruit choices in your meal plan into bread, meat and fat choices. Look back at page 56 if you have forgotten how to do this. And you can do all your figuring before the party.

Maybe you'd like to have your birthday party at home with a birthday cake and ice cream. You can do that, too!

Help your Mom or Dad bake a birthday cake that doesn't have a lot of sugar in it. They may have a cookbook with recipes for cakes that boys and girls with diabetes can eat.

Or, you can use the cake recipe on the next page and serve it with ice cream. Remember, since it is your birthday, you can have 1/2 cup of ice cream or ice milk.

Play some running games after everyone eats to help keep your blood sugar down.

Chocolate Pear Cake

1 square with topping = 1 bread/starch + 1 fat

1 1/2 cup cake flour

1 1/2 teaspoons baking powder

1/4 teaspoon baking soda

1/4 teaspoon salt

1/3 cup margarine

1/2 cup granulated sugar

2 ounces unsweetened chocolate

1/2 cup low-cholesterol egg substitute

5 unsweetened canned pear halves, mashed

1/2 cup light sour cream

1/2 teaspoon vanilla extract

Sift cake flour with baking powder, baking soda, and salt. In another bowl, cream margarine, add sugar and beat until fluffy. Melt unsweetened chocolate over hot water in a double boiler. Cool chocolate slightly and add to margarine/sugar mixture. Mix well. Blend in egg substitute and mashed pear. Add light sour cream and vanilla. Add sifted dry ingredients in two or three parts, mixing well after each addition.

Spray a 9" x 13" pan with non-stick spray. Pour mixture into pan and bake 20 to 25 minutes at 350 degrees. Cut into 24 squares. Serve each piece with two tablespoons of non-dairy whipped topping and a candle.

BIRTHDAY PARTIES, HALLOWEEN, AND OTHER STUFF

A friend's birthday party

Finding the right food to eat at a friend's birthday party is often harder than at your own party. You don't get to choose what treats to serve.

A good friend's birthday is special, though. So you can have a special treat as long as you don't eat too much. The list on this page shows some treats you might find at the birthday party of a good friend. You can eat one or two of these treats, but don't eat more than the amount listed.

And, if possible, use them in place of your regular snack.

To keep your blood sugar from going too high, exercise when you get home from the party. This will help your body use up the extra sugar in your blood.

These treats equal **1 bread/starch**

Angel food cake, small piece	1
Lady fingers	2
Vanilla or chocolate pudding (regular)	1/4 cup

These treats equal **1 bread/starch + 1 fat**

Cookie, 3 inch diameter	1
Cookie, 1 3/4 inch diameter	2
Cupcake, plain, no frosting	1
Ice milk	1/2 cup
Lorna Doone™ shortbread	3

These treats equal **1 bread/starch + 2 fat.**

Brownie (no icing 3 x 2 x 1 inch square)	1
Cheetos™	1 ounce
Corn chips	1 ounce
Donut holes plain, cake type or raised	3
Doritos™, tortilla chips	1 ounce
Ice cream	1/2 cup
Potato chips	1 ounce
Potato sticks	1 ounce

BIRTHDAY PARTIES, HALLOWEEN, AND OTHER STUFF

Halloween

Diabetes won't stop you from trick-or-treating with your friends on Halloween.

You shouldn't eat the candy people put in your trick-or-treat bag, but you can use treats like nuts, trail mix, granola bars, plain cookies, chips, and fruit. Save them and use them for snacks the rest of the week.

Invite some of your friends to your house after trick-or-treating for some treats. That will also help you take care of your diabetes.

See the Halloween Treats list. You can use the treat for your evening snack.

Play some games before your friends go home. You may use some of the candy in your trick-or-treat bag for prizes, or give it to a children's hospital in your town.

You can also set up a Halloween Trading Post with your Mom, Dad, Grandma, Grandpa, or a special adult. Arrange to trade your candy for something you want. For example:

- 3 candy bars = 1 TV show
- 4 candy bars = 1 late TV show
- 5 candy bars = 1 movie
- 3 of any item = 35 cents
- 6 of any item = $1.25
- 7 of any item = a new game

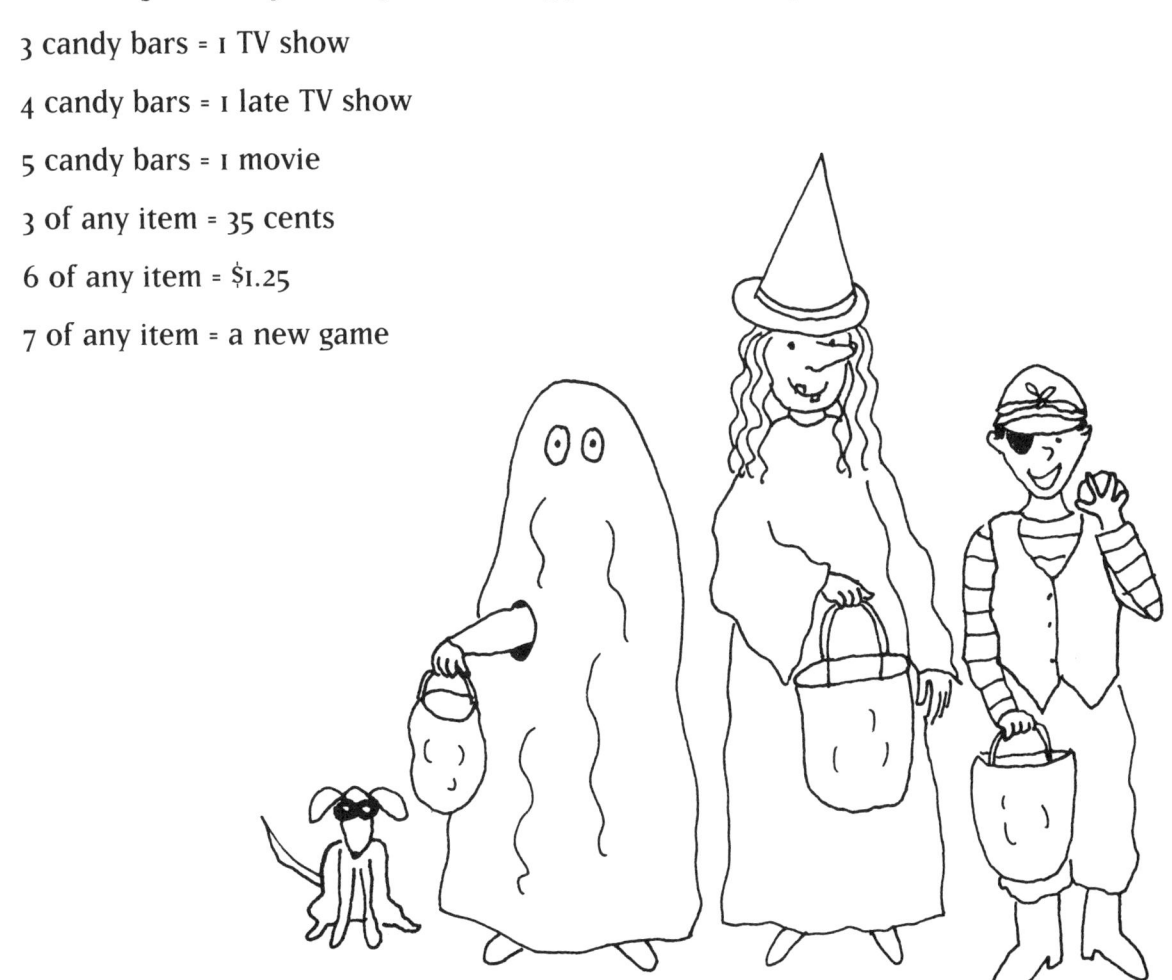

BIRTHDAY PARTIES, HALLOWEEN, AND OTHER STUFF

HALLOWEEN TREATS

YOGURT SUNDAE

Mix 1 choice of fresh fruit and 1 cup of plain yogurt* in sundae glasses.
1 sundae = 1 milk + 1 fruit

SNACK-A-BOBS

Put 1 ounce of cheese cubes and 1 ounce of meat slices on skewers.
1 snack-a-bob = 2 meat

RAISIN-NUT POPCORN

Mix 1 cup of hot-air-popped popcorn with 2 tablespoons of raisins and 10 whole peanuts. **1 serving = 1/3 bread/starch + 1 fruit + 1 fat**

APPLE CHIPS

Slice 1 whole apple and place on a lightly greased pan. Bake at 325 degrees for 20 minutes or until dry. Store in an air-tight container.
1 apple = 1 fruit

SMALL PIZZAS

Top 1/2 of an English muffin with tomato sauce, basil, oregano, and pepper. Sprinkle with 1 ounce of part-skim mozzarella cheese. Broil until brown and bubbly. **1 pizza = 1 meat + 1 bread/starch + 1 vegetable**

*Sweeten plain yogurt, if desired, with Equal® or 2 to 3 teaspoons of sugar-free gelatin powder.

BIRTHDAY PARTIES, HALLOWEEN, AND OTHER STUFF

School parties

Does you class at school have a party once in a while? Maybe on Valentine's day or when someone has a birthday? You can enjoy them, but you have to be careful.

Sometimes treats are served which will make your blood sugar go up quickly, so you have to plan ahead.

Ask your parents to have your teacher let them know when there is going to be a party. Then they can find out what treats are planned. Your teacher may even be willing to have the party at your regular snack time.

If you can't eat the treats being planned, maybe your parents will send some extra food you can eat and share with your friends.

Some of the treats we listed for your Halloween party would be fun. So would the Oatmeal Raisin Bars on the next page. You and your parents will think of others. Maybe your treats will be the best food at the party!

Oatmeal Raisin Bars

1 bar = 1 bread/starch + 1 fruit + 1 fat

1/3 cup margarine

1/4 cup dark brown sugar, packed (it's O.K.!)

1 1/2 cup EggBeaters®

1/2 cup buttermilk

2 tablespoons dark molasses

1 tablespoon vanilla

1 package dry Butter Buds®

1/2 cup whole wheat flour

1/2 cup all-purpose flour

1 cup unprocessed bran

3 cups rolled oats, uncooked

1 teaspoon baking powder

1/2 teaspoon baking soda

1/2 teaspoon salt (optional)

1 tablespoon cinnamon

1 cup raisins

Cream margarine and brown sugar together. Blend in EggBeaters, buttermilk, molasses, vanilla and Butter Buds. Add flours, bran, oats, baking powder, baking soda, salt, cinnamon and raisins. Mix well. Spread mixture evenly in a 9" x 13" pan sprayed with non-stick spray. Bake 15 minutes at 350 degrees. Cool and cut into 16 bars.

BIRTHDAY PARTIES, HALLOWEEN, AND OTHER STUFF

Slumber parties

Don't miss the fun of a slumber party at the home of a friend. Ask your parents to talk with your friend's parents about what treats will be served, and about the best time for you to eat.

Use the treats for your evening snack.

If you can't eat the treats that are being served, take your own. And take some extras for your friends. A great treat to take for yourself and your friends is Banana-Peanut Pinwheels.

BANANA-PEANUT PINWHEELS

4 rounds = 1 fruit + 1/2 high-fat meat

1 banana

2 tablespoons peanut butter

1. Slice the banana in half, lengthwise. Be careful not to break the banana halves.
2. Spread the cut side of each half with 1/2 tablespoon of peanut butter.
3. Press the cut sides back together, firmly.
4. Slice the banana in half again, lengthwise. The banana will now be cut into quarters, lengthwise, but two of the quarters will be stuck together with peanut butter.
5. Again spread the cut sides with peanut putter and press together. The whole banana is now back together.
6. Chill slightly in the refrigerator and then slice into 1 inch thick rounds.

BIRTHDAY PARTIES, HALLOWEEN, AND OTHER STUFF

Camping trips

Pitch those tents! Gather the firewood! Break out the hamburgers! Slap the mosquitoes! Sure, you can go camping.

Choosing the right things and the correct amounts from the foods served on most camping trips should be easy for you. Most of the foods will be things you eat at home.

You already know how to fit hamburgers, buns, baked potatoes, carrot sticks, corn on the cob, apples, bananas, cereals, pancakes, and lots of other foods into your meal plan.

Just to make sure, ask ahead of time what meals are being planned. Better still, volunteer to help plan the meals so you'll know ahead of time what foods will be served.

Figure out before the camping trip what you can eat and how much, and be sure to take lots of snacks with you. The list on the next page may help.

If hiking up a mountain, lots of swimming or other hard exercise are part of your camping trip, you will need extra snacks.

Review the exercise chart on page 65 before your camping trip. It will remind you about when you need extra snacks.

GOOD SNACKS FOR A CAMPING TRIP

Peanut butter sandwich crackers, trail mix, granola bars, nuts

Lipton's Cup-o-Soup®

Beef jerky

Tuna fish, salmon in flip-top cans

Cheese wrapped in cellophane

Crackers, bread

Muffins — corn, bran

Dried fruit — apricots, apples, prunes

Seeds — sunflower, pumpkin

Juice-in-a-box (4-ounce box)

BIRTHDAY PARTIES, HALLOWEEN, AND OTHER STUFF

Thanksgiving and other holidays

Great smells from the kitchen, two days off from school, maybe a football game—it's Thanksgiving day and of course you'll want to join in the fun of good eating. Most of the food should be no problem.

Review the food lists on pages 83–107 to find out how much you should eat. And follow your meal plan as closely as possible.

Be careful with desserts, however. Your family may have a special treat always served on Thanksgiving or some other holiday. Like grandma's pumpkin pie. Your parents may call your dietitian to find out if you can fit a piece into your meal plan.

Exercise after dinner will help your body use up the extra sugar. Better still, ask grandma or grandpa to use the pumpkin pie recipe printed on the next page.

Special Pumpkin Pie

1/8 of pie = 2 bread/starch + 1 fat

1/10 of pie = 1 bread/starch + 1/2 milk = 1 fat

2 cups cooked or canned pumpkin

1 1/2 cups undiluted evaporated skim milk

3 tablespoons dark brown sugar (It's O.K.!)

2 tablespoons white sugar (It's O.K., too!)

1/4 teaspoon salt

1 teaspoon cinnamon

1/2 teaspoon ginger

1/4 teaspoon nutmeg or allspice

1/8 teaspoon cloves

1/2 cup low-cholesterol egg substitute

Mix ingredients until well blended. Pour into pie crust (commercial is fine). Bake 15 minutes at 425 degrees, then reduce heat to 350 degrees and bake about 45 minutes or until an inserted knife comes out clean.

FOOD LISTS

MILK LIST

BEST CHOICES:

Nonfat (skim) or low-fat selections.

BE SURE:

You get 3 to 4 servings per day to get enough calcium in your diet.

ITEM	PORTION
Nonfat milk (skim)	1 c.
Low-fat milk (1/2%)	1 c.
Nonfat yogurt made with NutraSweet® such as Yoplait® Light, Columbo® Slender Spoonfuls™, and Dannon® Light	6-8 oz.
Lactaid® milk (skim)	1 c.
Powdered, nonfat milk (before adding liquid)	1/3 c.
Canned, evaporated skim milk	1/2 c.
* Sugar-free hot cocoa mix plus 6 oz. of water	1 c.
Sugar-free pudding made with nonfat or low-fat milk	1/2 c.

NONFAT SELECTIONS

One choice provides:
Calories: 80
Protein: 8 gms
Carb: 12 gms
Fat: 0 gms

* Most cocoa mixes do not provide the same amount of calcium as one cup of milk. Mixes that do provide the same amount should indicate on the label that the product contains 30% Reference Daily Intakes (RDIs) for calcium. An example of a product that meets these calcium requirements is Alba® sugar-free, hot cocoa mix.

MILK LIST

LOW-FAT SELECTIONS

One choice provides:
Calories: 107
Protein: 8 gms
Carb: 12 gms
Fat: 3 gms

ITEM	PORTION
Low-fat milk (1%)	1 c.
Yogurt, plain, unflavored	1 c.
Lactaid® milk (1%)	1 c.

MEDIUM- AND HIGH-FAT

One choice provides:
Calories: 125-150
Protein: 8 gms
Carb: 12 gms
Fat: 5-8 gms

The following milk items should be used sparingly for children 2 years of age or older because of the high saturated fat and cholesterol content. It is generally recommended that children under the age of 2 years continue to drink whole milk. Consult your child's pediatrician for further advice.

ITEM	PORTION
Low-fat milk (2%)	1 c.
Whole milk	1 c.

VEGETABLE LIST

BEST CHOICES:

Fresh or raw vegetables: dark green, leafy or orange.

BE SURE:

To choose at least 2 vegetables each day.

WE ENCOURAGE:

Steaming with a minimum amount of water. Also, fresh and frozen vegetables are lower in salt than canned vegetables, unless the canned product states "low sodium."

ITEM	PORTION
Artichoke	1/2
Asparagus	1 c.
Bamboo shoots	1/2 c.
Bean sprouts	1/2 c.
Beets	1/2 c.
Beet greens	1 c.
*† Broccoli	1/2 c.
*† Brussel sprouts	1/2 c.
* Cabbage	1 c.
† Carrots	1/2 c.
* Cauliflower	1 c.
Celery	1 c.
* Collard greens	1 c.
Eggplant	1/2 c.
Fennel leaf	1 c.
Green beans	1 c.
* Green pepper	1 c.
* Kale	1/2 c.

One choice provides:
Calories: 28
Protein: 2 gms
Carb: 5 gms
Fat: 0 gms

* Good source of vitamin C
† Good source of vitamin A

VEGETABLE LIST

ITEM	PORTION
Kohlrabi	1/2 c.
Leeks	1/2 c.
Mushrooms, fresh	1 c.
Mustard greens, cooked	1 c.
Okra	1/2 c.
Onion	1/2 c.
Pea pods, Chinese (snow peas)	1/2 c.
Radishes	1 c.
* Red pepper	1 c.
Rutabagas	1/2 c.
* Sauerkraut	1/2 c.
† Spinach, cooked	1/2 c.
Squash	
summer	1 c.
zucchini	1 c.
Swiss chard	1 c.
*† Tomato (ripe)	1 medium
Tomato juice	1/2 c.
Tomato paste	1 1/2 Tbsp.
Tomato sauce, canned	1/3 c.
Turnips	1/2 c.
Vegetables, mixed	1/4 c.
V-8 juice	1/2 c.
Wax beans	1 c.
Water chestnuts	5 whole

Because of their low carbohydrate and calorie content, the following RAW vegetables may be used liberally.

Alfalfa sprouts	Lettuce
Chicory	Parsley
Chinese cabbage	Pickles (unsweetened)
Cucumber	Pimiento
Endive	† Spinach
Escarole	Watercress

* Good source of vitamin C
† Good source of vitamin A

FRUIT LIST

BEST CHOICES:

Fresh whole fruit with peel whenever possible.

BE SURE:

To choose at least 2 to 3 servings per day of fresh, frozen, or canned fruit packed in its own juice or water with no added sugar.

ITEM	PORTION
Apple, 2 in. diameter	1 small
Apple, dried	1/4 c.
Applesauce, unsweetened	1/2 c.
† Apricots,	
fresh	4 medium
canned	4 halves
dried	7 halves
Banana, 9 in. length, peeled	1/2
Banana flakes or chips	3 Tbsp.
* Blackberries	3/4 c.
* Blueberries	3/4 c.
* Boysenberries	1 c.
Canned fruit,	
unless otherwise stated	1/2 c.
*† Cantaloupe, 5 in. diameter	
sectioned	1/3 melon
cubed	1 c.
*† Casaba, 7 in. diameter	
sectioned	1/6 melon
cubed	1 1/3 c.
Cherries, sweet fresh	12

One choice provides:
Calories: 60
Protein: 0 gms
Carb: 15 gms
Fat: 0 gms

* Good source of vitamin C
† Good source of vitamin A

FRUIT LIST

ITEM	PORTION
Dates	3
Figs	2 small
Fruit cocktail, no sugar added	1/2 c.
*Grapefruit, 4 in. diameter	1/2
Grapes	15 small
Guava	1 1/2 small
*† Honeydew melon, 6 1/2 in. diameter	
sectioned	1/8 melon
cubed	1 c.
*† Kiwi (3 oz.)	1 large
Kumquat	5 medium
* Lemon	1 large
Loquats, fresh	12
Lychees, fresh or dried	10
*† Mango	1/2 small
sliced	1/2 c.
* Nectarine, 2 1/2 in. diameter	1
* Orange, 3 in. diameter	1
*† Papaya, 3 1/2 in. diameter	
sectioned	1/2
cubed	1 c.
† Peach, 2 1/2 in. diameter	1
Pear	1 small
Persimmon,	
native	2
Japanese, 2 1/2 in. diameter	1/2
Pineapple,	
fresh, diced	3/4 c.
canned	1/3 c.
Plantain, cooked	1/3 c.
Plum, 2 in. diameter	2
Pomegranate, 3 1/2 in. diameter	1/2
Prunes, dried, medium	3

* Good source of vitamin C
† Good source of vitamin A

FRUIT LIST

ITEM	PORTION
Raisins	2 Tbsp.
* Raspberries	1 c.
Rhubarb, fresh, diced	3 c.
* Strawberries	1 1/3 c.
* Tangerine, 2 1/2 in. diameter	2
* Watermelon, diced	1 1/4 c.

FRUIT JUICE

NOTE:

Fruit juice may raise blood sugar rapidly, especially when eaten on an empty stomach or with a small amount of food such as a snack. Limit your intake of juice to no more than one meal each day or to times when you are playing hard or treating a low blood sugar. Certain juices or juice blends are low in vitamin C, such as apple juice. Choose vitamin C (ascorbic acid) fortified varieties. A 4-oz. fruit juice box is equal to one fruit choice.

ITEM	PORTION
Apple cider	3 oz.
Apple juice, unsweetened	4 oz.
Cranapple, low-calorie	12 oz.
Cranberry, low-calorie	10 oz.
Grape juice, unsweetened	4 oz.
* Grapefruit juice, unsweetened	5 oz.
Lemon juice, unsweetened	6 oz.
* Orange juice, unsweetened	4 oz.
Pineapple juice, unsweetened	4 oz.
Prune juice, unsweetened	3 oz.

* Good source of vitamin C
† Good source of vitamin A

BREAD/STARCH LIST

BEST CHOICES:
Whole grain breads and cereals, dried beans and peas.

BE SURE:
Cereals contain less than 5 grams of sucrose per serving.
(In general, one bread choice equals 1 oz. of bread).

BREADS

One choice provides:
Calories: 80
Protein: 3 gms
Carb: 15 gms
Fat: trace

ITEM	PORTION
White, whole wheat, rye, etc.	1 slice
Raisin	1 slice
Italian and French	1 slice
Reduced calorie	
(1 slice equals 35 to 40 calories)	2 slices
Syrian	
pocket, 6 in. diameter	1/2 pocket
mini-pocket	1 pocket
Bagel	1/2 medium
English muffin	1/2 medium
Rolls	
bulkie	1/2 small
dinner, plain	1 small
frankfurter	1/2 medium
hamburger	1/2 medium
Bread crumbs	3 Tbsp.

CEREALS

ITEM	PORTION
Cooked cereals (for example, oatmeal, farina)	1/2 c.
Bran	
† All Bran with Extra Fiber™	1 c.
† All Bran™	1/3 c.
† 100% Bran™	2/3 c.

BREAD/STARCH LIST

ITEM	PORTION
† 40% Bran Flakes™	1/2 c.
† Bran Chex™	1/2 c.
† Fiber One™	2/3 c.
Cheerios™	1 c.
Common Sense Oat Bran™	1/2 c.
Corn, Rice Chex™	2/3 c.
Cornflakes™	3/4 c.
Crispix™	1/2 c.
Fortified Oat Flakes™	1/2 c.
Granola™	1/4 c. = 1 bread + 1 fat
Grapenuts™	3 Tbsp.
† Grapenut Flakes™	2/3 c.
Just Right™	1/2 c.
Kenmei Rice Bran™	1/2 c.
Kix™	1 c.
Nutrigrain™	1/2 c.
Product 19™	1/2 c.
Puffed Rice, Wheat™	1 1/2 c.
Raisin bran	1/2 c.
Rice Krispies™	3/4 c.
† Shredded Wheat™ biscuit	1
spoon size	1/2 c.
† Shredded Wheat n'Bran™	1/2 c.
Special K™	3/4 c.
Strawberry Squares®	1/3 c.
Team™	2/3 c.
Total™	3/4 c.
Triples®	1/2 c.
† Wheat Chex™	1/2 c.
† Wheaties™	2/3 c.
+ Other cold cereals	2/3 c.

† Cereals high in fiber.
+ To determine the appropriateness of other cereals, read the side panel on the container. If the number listed next to grams of sucrose is 5 or less, it is an acceptable choice. Ask your dietitian if you have questions about portion sizes for cereals not listed.

BREAD/STARCH LIST

STARCHY VEGETABLES

ITEM	PORTION
Corn	1/2 c.
Corn on the cob, 5 inches long	1
Lima beans	1/2 c.
Parsnips	1/2 c.
Peas, green, canned or frozen	2/3 c.
Plantain, cooked	1/3 c.
* Potato, white	
mashed	1/2 c.
baked	1/2 medium or 1 small (3 oz.)
*† Sweet potato	
mashed	1/3 c.
baked	1/2 medium (2 oz.)
† Pumpkin	3/4 c.
† Winter squash, acorn or butternut	3/4 c.

* Good source of vitamin C
† Good source of vitamin A

PASTA (cooked)

ITEM	PORTION
Macaroni, noodles, spaghetti (one ounce dry pasta makes 1/2 c. cooked pasta)	1/2 c.

LEGUMES

ITEM	PORTION
Beans, peas, lentil (dried and cooked)	1/3 c.
Baked beans, canned, no pork (vegetarian style)	1/3 c.

GRAINS

ITEM	PORTION
Barley, cooked	1/4 c.
Bulgur, cooked	1/3 c.

BREAD/STARCH LIST

ITEM	PORTION
Cornmeal	2 1/2 Tbsp.
Cornstarch	2 Tbsp.
Flour	3 Tbsp.
Kasha, cooked	1/3 c.
Rice, cooked	1/3 c.
Wheat germ	1/4 c. = 1 bread + 1 lean meat

BEST CHOICES:

Lower salt products, such as saltines with unsalted tops.

SNACKS, CRACKERS, AND PLAIN COOKIES
(Equal to one bread choice)

ITEM	PORTION
AK-mak™, regular and sesame	4 crackers
Animal crackers	8
Crokine™ puffed crispbread	4
Finn Crisp™	4
Gingersnaps	3
Graham crackers, 2 1/2 in. squares	3
Krispen™ crispbread	4
Matzoh or matzoh with bran	1 (3/4 oz.) board
Manischewitz™ whole wheat matzoh crackers	7
Melba toast rectangles	5
Melba toast rounds	10
Norwegian flatbread such as Kavli™	
thin	3
thick	2
Popcorn, popped, no fat added	3 c.
Pretzel	3/4 oz.
Mr. Phipps™ pretzel chips	12
Rice cakes, popcorn cakes	2
Mini rice cakes	8
Rye Krisp™, triple crackers	3

BREAD/STARCH LIST

ITEM	PORTION
Ryvita™ crisp breads	4
Saltines	6
Snack Well's® Cinnamon Grahams	12
Social Teas™	4
Stella D'Oro Almond Toast™	1 1/2
Stella D'Oro Egg Biscuit™	2
Stoned Wheat Thins™	2 1/2
Tortilla, Guiltless Gourmet®, no oil tortilla chip™	8
Uneedas™	4
Wasa Lite or Golden Type or Hearty RyeCrisp Bread™	2
Vegetable Garden Crisps™	9
Zwieback™	3

SNACKS, CRACKERS, AND PLAIN COOKIES FOR OCCASIONAL USE
(Equal to one bread *plus one fat choice*)

ITEM	PORTION
Arrowroot™	4
Bordeaux Cookies™, Pepperidge Farm	3
Butter crackers	
rounds	7
rectangular	6
Cheez-Its™	27
Cheez Nips™	20
Club or Townhouse Crackers™	6
Combos™	1 oz.
Corn chips	15 = 1 bread + 2 fats
Escort Crackers™	5
Girl Scout Cookies® Trefoils™	4
Goldfish™, Pepperidge Farm	36
Granola bar, plain, raisin or peanut butter (such as, Nature Valley®)	1
Lorna Doones™	3
Meal Mates™	5

BREAD/STARCH LIST

ITEM	PORTION
Munch 'ems™	23
Oyster crackers	24
Peanut butter sandwich crackers	3
Potato chips	15 = 1 bread + 2 fat
Ritz™	7
Sea Rounds™	2
Smart Food® Light	1 oz.
Sociables™	9
Stella D'Oro Seasame Breadsticks™	2
Stella D'Oro Breakfast Treats™	1
Stella D'Oro Golden Bar™	1
Stella D'Oro Lady Stella Assortment™	3
Sunshine Hi Ho's™	6
Teddy Grahams® (any flavor)	15
Tidbits™	21
Triscuits™	5
Vanilla Wafers™	6
Wasa Fiber Plus Crisp Bread™	4
Wasa Sesame™ or Breakfast Crisp Bread™	2
Waverly Wafers™	6
Wheat Thins™	12
Wheatables®	22

MEAT LIST

BEST CHOICES:
Nonfat or low-fat selections.

BE SURE:
To trim off visible fat.

Bake, broil, roast, or steam selections. Remove skin from poultry (chicken and turkey) or eat skinless poultry. Weigh your portion after cooking. Raw meat will lose 1/4 of its weight with cooking. For example: 1 lb. (16 oz.) raw meat yields 12 oz. cooked meat; 4 oz. raw meat yields 3 oz. cooked meat, etc.

NONFAT SELECTIONS

One choice provides:
Calories: 40-45
Protein: 7 gms
Carb: 0 gms
Fat: 0 gms

ITEM	PORTION
Nonfat cheese products:	
* Alpine Lace Free'n Lean Cheese™	1 oz.
* Hood Free cottage cheese™	1/4 c.
* Calabro™ 100% skim ricotta	1 oz.
* Kraft® Free® Singles	1 oz.

* High in salt.

LOW-FAT SELECTIONS

One choice provides:
Calories: 55
Protein: 7 gms
Carb: 0 gms
Fat: 3 gms

ITEM	PORTION
Cheese:	
Cottage, 1% fat	1/4 c.
* Lite-Line cheese™, * Nuform cheese™, Weight Watcher's cheese™, Laughing Cow™, Kraft® Healthy Favorites™	1 oz.
Cooked dried beans	1/2 c. = 1 meat + 1 bread
Egg substitute with less than 55 calories per 1/4 c.	1/2 c.
Egg whites	3

MEAT LIST

ITEM	PORTION
Fish and seafood:	
Fresh or frozen	1 oz.
Canned:	
Herring, uncreamed or *smoked	1 oz.
Imitation crab	1 oz.
Sardines, drained	3
Water packed clams, oysters, scallops, ***shrimp	1 oz.
Water packed salmon, tuna, crab, ***lobster	1/4 c.
Hotdogs or franks, 97% fat-free, such as Healthy Choice™ Jumbo Franks, Oscar Mayer® Healthy Favorites™, Hormel® Light & Lean®	1 oz.
* Luncheon meat, 95% fat-free	1 oz.
Healthy Choice™ 96% fat-free	
Ground Beef	1 oz.
Turkey Sausage	1 oz.
Poultry: chicken, turkey or cornish hen, without skin	1 oz.
Ground chicken, turkey meat	1 oz.
* Canadian bacon	1 oz.
† Tofu	3 oz.

* High in salt.
*** People trying to reduce dietary cholesterol may need to limit these. For additional information ask your dietitian.
† Good source of dietary calcium.

ITEM	PORTION
Veal, except for breast	1 oz.
Pork, except for deviled ham, ground pork, and spare ribs	1 oz.
Bacon, Healthy Choice™ turkey bacon	2 strips

MEDIUM-FAT SELECTIONS

One choice provides:
Calories: 75
Protein: 7 gms
Carb: 0 gms
Fat: 5 gms

MEAT LIST

ITEM	PORTION
Beef, chipped, chuck, flank steak, hamburger with 15% fat, rib eye, rump, sirloin, tenderloin top and bottom round	1 oz.
Lamb, except for breast	1 oz.
Cheese:	
† Part-skim mozzarella and mozzarella cheese sticks, † Part-skim ricotta, Farmer, Neufchâtel, Velveeta® Light, Tasty-Lo® sharp cheddar cheese spread, Jarlsberg Light, Dormans® Slim Jack reduced-fat Monterey, Cracker Barrel™ Light, Cabot® Light Vitalait™, Kraft® Light	1 oz.
* Parmesan, * Romano	3 Tbsp.
** Egg	1
Egg substitute with 56-80 calories per 1/4 c.	1/4 c.
* Luncheon meat, 86% fat free	1 oz.
Turkey bacon	2 slices
Peanut butter	1 Tbsp. = 1 meat + 1 fat

* High in salt.
** Eggs are high in cholesterol. Limit consumption to 3-4 per week.
† Good source of dietary calcium.

MEAT LIST

BE SURE:

Because of the high saturated fat and cholesterol content, the meat choices listed below should be used sparingly.

ITEM	PORTION
Beef:	
brisket, club and rib steak, * corned beef, regular hamburger with 20% fat, rib roast, short ribs	1 oz.
Hotdog or frank	1 = 1 high-fat meat + 1 fat
Lamb breast	1 oz.
Pork:	
* deviled ham, ground pork, spare ribs, * sausage (patty or link)	1 oz.
Veal breast	1 oz.
Poultry:	
capon, duck, goose	1 oz.
Regular cheese:	
*† American, Brie, † cheddar, Colby, * feta, † Monterey Jack, † Swiss, Muenster, provolone	1 oz.
* Luncheon meats:	
bologna, bratwurst, braunschweiger, knockwurst, liverwurst, pastrami, Polish sausage, salami, Spam®	1 oz.
Organ meats:	
liver, heart, kidney	1 oz.
Fried fish	1 oz.

* High in salt.
† Good source of dietary calcium.

HIGH-FAT SELECTIONS

One choice provides:
Calories: 100
Protein: 7 gms
Carb: 0 gms
Fat: 8 gms

FAT LIST

BEST CHOICES:

More unsaturated selections.

BE SURE:

When using low calorie version of fat choices, use amounts equal to 45 calories for one serving.

One choice provides:
Calories: 45
Protein: 0 gms
Carb: 0 gms
Fat: 5 gms

ITEM	PORTION
Avocado, 4 in. diameter	1/8
D-Zerta™ whipped topping	5 Tbsp.
Margarine, soft tub	1 tsp.
Reduced calories	1 Tbsp.
† Mayonnaise	1 tsp.
Reduced calories	1 Tbsp.
Nondairy creamer, liquid	2 Tbsp.
Nondairy creamer, lite, liquid	5 Tbsp.
Nuts:	
Almonds	6 whole
Brazil	2 medium
Cashews	5-8 whole
Filberts (hazelnuts)	5 whole
Macadamia	3 whole
Peanuts	
Spanish	20 whole
Virginia	10 whole
Pecans	2 whole
Pignoli (pine nuts)	1 Tbsp.
Pistachio	12 whole
Walnuts	2 whole
Other	1 Tbsp.

FAT LIST

ITEM	PORTION
Oils:	
Corn, cottonseed, olive, peanut (monounsaturated), safflower, soy, sunflower	1 tsp.
* Olives:	
green	5 small
black	2 large
Salad dressings:	
*† French, Italian	1 Tbsp.
Mayonnaise type	2 tsp.
* Seeds (without shells)	
sesame, sunflower	1 Tbsp.
pumpkin	2 tsp.

* High in salt.
† Can be used in a cholesterol-reducing diet if made with corn, cottonseed, safflower, soy, or sunflower oil as the first ingredient.

MORE SATURATED

ITEM	PORTION
Butter	1 tsp.
Bacon, crisp	1 strip
Chitterlings	1/2 oz.
Coconut, shredded	2 Tbsp.
Coffee whitener, liquid	2 Tbsp.
Coffee whitener, powder	4 Tbsp.
Cool Whip™, regular or chocolate	3 Tbsp.
Cool Whip™ Lite	5 Tbsp.
Cream:	
Half and Half	2 Tbsp.
Heavy	1 Tbsp.
Light	1 1/2 Tbsp.
Sour	2 Tbsp.
Whipped, fluid	1 Tbsp.
Whipped, pressurized topping	1/3 c.

FAT LIST

ITEM	PORTION
Cream cheese	1 Tbsp.
Whipped	2 Tbsp.
Lard	1 tsp.
Margarine, stick	1 tsp.
Oils:	
Palm, coconut	1 tsp.
Salad dressings:	
(Oil not listed as first ingredient)	
*French, Italian	1 Tbsp.
Mayonnaise type	2 tsp.
Salt pork	1/4 oz.

* High in salt.

MISCELLANEOUS LIST

Many foods are made up of several food groups. These mixed foods can be incorporated into your meal plan by substituting them for choices from more than one food group.

*CANNED SOUP

ITEM	PORTION	FOOD CHOICE
Rice or noodles with broth prepared with water	8 oz.	1/2 bread, 1/2 fat
Chunky style, ready to serve	8 oz.	1 bread, 1 meat, 1 vegetable
Cream soup		
Made with water	8 oz.	1/2 bread, 1 1/2 fat
Made with 1% low-fat milk	8 oz.	1/2 bread, 1/2 milk, 1 1/2 fat
Clam Chowder, New England style, prepared with 1% low-fat milk	8 oz.	1/2 bread, 1 milk, 1 fat
Lentil with ham, ready to serve	8 oz.	1 bread, 1 meat, 1 vegetable
Minestrone, ready to serve	8 oz.	1 bread, 1 vegetable
Split pea with ham, ready to serve	8 oz.	2 bread, 1 1/2 meat
Tomato, made with water	8 oz.	1 bread

* High in salt unless specially canned without it.

PREPARED FOODS

ITEM	PORTION	FOOD CHOICE
Biscuit	2 in. diameter (1 oz.)	1 bread + 1 fat
Croissant	4 x 4 x 1 3/4 in.	1 bread + 2 fats
Cornbread	2 x 2 x 1 in.	1 bread + 1 fat
French toast (frozen)	2 slices	2 bread + 1 fat
Muffin, bran or corn	2 in. diameter (1 1/2 oz.)	1 1/2 bread + 1 fat

MISCELLANEOUS LIST

ITEM	PORTION	FOOD CHOICE
Pancake	4 in. diameter	2=1 bread + 1 fat
Waffle	4 in. diameter	1 bread + 1 fat
Eggowaffle Special K™	4 in. diameter	1 bread
Taco shells	2	1 bread + 1 fat
Taco with meat and cheese	1	2 meat, 1 bread, 1 fat
Tortilla:		
corn	6 in. diameter	2=1 bread + 1 fat
flour	7 in. diameter	1 bread + 1 fat
* Plain cheese pizza	1/8 of 14 in. diameter	1 bread, 1 meat, 1 vegetable, 1 fat
Lasagna, homemade	2 1/2 x 2 1/2 x 1 3/4 in.	1 bread, 3 meat, 2 vegetable, 1 fat
* Ravioli, canned	1 c.	1 bread, 1 meat, 1 vegetable
frozen	3 large	2 bread + 1 fat
Beef stew, homemade	1 c.	1 bread, 3 meat, 1 vegetable
Beef stew, canned	1 c.	1 bread + 1 meat
Chili with meat and beans, homemade	1 c.	2 bread + 3 meat
* Spaghetti, canned	1 c.	2 bread + 1 fat
with meat	1 c.	1 1/2 bread, 1 meat, 1 vegetable, 1 fat
Popcorn, microwave light	3 cups	1 bread + 1 fat
Potatoes, french fries, 2 to 3 1/2 in. length	10	1 bread + 2 fats
Stuffing mix, cooked	1/3 c.	1 bread + 1 fat
Potato or macaroni salad made with regular mayonnaise	1/2 c.	1 bread + 2 fats
* Ramen Noodles, all flavors, as prepared (for example, LaChoy®)	1/2 package	2 bread + 1 fat

* High salt unless specially prepared without it.

MISCELLANEOUS LIST

ITEM	PORTION	FOOD CHOICE
* Macaroni and Cheese, as prepared (for example, Kraft®)	3/4 c.	2 bread + 1/2 meat + 2 fats
Tater Tots®	3 oz.	1 bread + 1 fat

* High in salt.

DESSERTS

ITEM	PORTION	FOOD CHOICE
Ice cream	1/2 c.	1 bread + 2 fat
† Frozen iced milk	1/2 c.	1 bread + 1 fat
† Pudding, sugar-free made with nonfat or 1% low-fat milk	1/2 c.	1/2 milk + 1/2 bread

† Good source of dietary calcium.

FROZEN YOGURTS

BEST CHOICE:

Nonfat, sugar-free yogurt is recommended as the best choice because of its low-sugar, low-fat content.

ITEM	PORTION	FOOD CHOICE
Soft Serve, nonfat, sugar free Freshens®, Honey Hill Farms®, I Can't Believe It's Yogurt®, TCBY®	1/2 c.	1 bread
Soft Serve Columbo® low-fat, Dannon® nonfat, Everything Yogurt® nonfat & low-fat, Honey Hill Farms® nonfat, I Can't Believe It's Yogurt® nonfat	1/2 c.	1 bread
Soft Serve Columbo® nonfat, Dairy Queen® nonfat vanilla, Dannon® low-fat, Freshens® low-fat & nonfat, McDonalds®, TCBY® nonfat	1/2 c.	1 1/2 bread

FREE FOODS

BE SURE:

The following foods contain very few calories and may be used freely in your meal plan. Items marked with an asterisk(*) should not be used, however, if you are on a salt (sodium) restricted diet.

GENERAL

- * Bouillon cubes
- * Broth (clear)
- Butter substitutes, such as Butter Buds® and Molly McButter®
- Calorie-free soft drinks, preferably caffeine-free
- * Catsup (1 Tbsp. daily - calculated as part of the total daily calories)
- Coffee
- * Consommé
- Cranberries (unsweetened)
- Drink mixes, sugar-free (for example, Crystal Light®, Kool-Aid®, Tang®)
- Extracts (See next page)
- Herbs (See next page)
- Horseradish
- Lime juice
- Lemon/Lime rind
- * Mustard (prepared)
- Non-caloric sugar substitute
- Orange Rind
- * Pickles (unsweetened)
- Rennet tablets
- Seasonings and condiments (See next page)
- * Soy sauce
- Spices (See next page)
- * Steak sauce
- Tabasco sauce
- Taco sauce
- Tea, weak
- Unprocessed bran (1 Tbsp.)
- Vinegar (cider, white, apple, wine)
- Yeast (dry or cake)

* High in salt.

FREE FOODS

SPICES, HERBS, AND EXTRACTS

Allspice
Almond extract
Anise extract
Anise seed
Baking powder
* Baking soda
Basil
Bay leaf
Black cherry extract
* Bouillon cube
Butter flavoring
* Butter salt
Caraway seeds
Cardamon
* Celery salt (seeds, leaves)
Chives
Chocolate extract
Cilantro (Mexican coriander)
Cinnamon
Cloves
Cream of tartar
Cumin
Curry
Dill
Fennel

Garlic
Ginger
Lemon extract
Mace
Maple extract
Mint
Mustard (dry)
Nutmeg
Onion (1 Tbsp.)
Orange extract
Oregano
Paprika
Parsley
Pepper
Peppermint extract
Pimento
Poppy seed
Poultry seed
Poultry seasonings
Saffron
Sage
* Salt
Savory
Vanilla extract

* High in salt.

FOODS LIKELY TO CAUSE PROBLEMS

BE SURE:

Because of their high sugar content, the foods listed below are likely to cause problems with the management of your diabetes. While you may eventually be able to include some of the items in your meal plan, they should be avoided until you have discussed them with your dietitian or physician or unless they have been recommended for treating insulin reactions.

** Alcohol: sweet wines, liqueur, cordials
Candy
Carbonated beverages containing sugar (including "natural" sodas)
Cereal (sugar coated)
Chewing gum (regular)
Desserts containing sugar:
    Cake
    Cookies with fillings or frosting
Gelatin dessert, regular
Fructose
Fruited yogurt, regular
Honey
Ice cream and ice milk including sodas and sundaes
Jam and jelly, regular
Marmalade
Pastries
Pie
Pudding, regular
Preserves, regular
Sherbet
Special "dietetic foods"
Sugar
Sugar-sweetened fruit drinks (Kool Aid®, Hi-C™, etc.)
Sweetened condensed milk
Syrups (maple, molasses, etc.)

LOW- OR REDUCED-CALORIE FOODS

BE SURE:

The labels of some foods contain the phrases "low calorie" or "reduced in calories". They will also state the number of calories per serving. Try to limit the use of these foods, which contain no more than 25 calories per serving, to three times a day. Always read the labels carefully before using these products. Consult your physician or dietitian if you plan to use them regularly.

Some lower calorie foods you may use in limited quantities are:

   diet and sugar-free jams/jellies - 1 tsp.,
   diet syrups,
   sugar-free hard candy,
   sugar-free gelatin mixes,
   sugar-free gum,
   nonfat salad dressing or
      fat-free mayonnaise - 2 Tbsp.
   sour cream alternative - 2 Tbsp.
   sugar-free popsicles

SUGAR, SWEETENERS, AND SWEETS

The names of most sweeteners available today appear in the chart below. Alongside the name of each sweetener are other names or "aliases" by which they are also known. The chart also indicates which of the sweeteners may be used, those that should be used with caution and those that should be avoided. Check with your physician or dietitian before using any of the sweeteners the chart indicates should not be used.

Use this chart to help you make decisions when evaluating and selecting sweeteners.

STOP - Do not use
CAUTION - Use with caution
GO - OK to use

NON-NUTRITIVE SWEETENER (NON-CALORIC)	ALIAS	ACTION	COMMENTS/ APPLICATIONS
ASPARTAME	Equal® SweetMate®	GO	180 times sweeter than sucrose. Loses sweetening effect when heated. Not accceptable for use in baking/cooking. Acceptable for use during pregnancy.
SACCHARIN	Sucaryl® Sugar Twin® Sweet Magic® Sweet'n Low®	GO	375 times sweeter than sucrose. Can be used in baking and cooking.
ACESULFAME-K	Sweet One™ Swiss Sweet™	GO	200 times sweeter than sucrose. Can be used in baking and cooking.

SUGAR, SWEETENERS, AND SWEETS

NUTRITIVE SWEETENER (CALORIC)	ALIAS	ACTION	COMMENTS/ APPLICATIONS
CAROB	Carob flour Carob powder Carob tips	STOP	75% sucrose, glucose and/or fructose. Tastes like chocolate.
CHOCOLATE	Bittersweet, Bitter, Milk chocolate	STOP	40-43% sucrose.
FRUCTOSE	Fruit sugar Levulose	CAUTION	100% fruit sugar.
GLUCOSE	Corn sugar Dextrose Grape sugar	STOP	Not as sweet as sucrose.
HONEY	Creamed honey Honey Comb	STOP	About 35% glucose, 40% fructose plus water.
LACTOSE	Milk sugar	CAUTION	50% glucose. Not as sweet as sucrose.
MALTOSE		STOP	100% glucose. Not as sweet as sucrose.
MOLASSES	Black Strap Golden syrup Refiners sugar	STOP	50-75% sucrose and invert sugar.

SUGAR, SWEETENERS, AND SWEETS

NUTRITIVE SWEETENER (CALORIC)	ALIAS	ACTION	COMMENTS/ APPLICATIONS
SUCROSE	Beet sugar Brown sugar Cane sugar Confectioner's sugar Invert sugar Powdered sugar Raw sugar Table sugar Turbinado	STOP	50% glucose. 50% fructose.
SUGAR ALCOHOL	Ducitol Mannitol Sorbitol Xylitol Hydrogenated starch hydrolysate	CAUTION	Not as sweet as sucrose. May cause diarrhea.
SYRUPS	Corn syrup Corn syrup solids and/or fructose High fructose syrups Honey Maple syrup Molasses Sugar cane sugar Sorghum syrup	STOP	Primarily glucose.

GUIDE FOR USE OF SUGAR SUBSTITUTES IN PLACE OF SUGAR

With most recipes, you can reduce the sugar by at least one-third without changing the taste and texture. For example, if the recipe calls for 1 cup of sugar, use 2/3 of a cup instead. Alternatively you may choose to reduce sugar intake by using artificial sweeteners. Aspartame (Equal® or Sweet Mate®) can be used in recipes that will be baked for less than 20 minutes. Don't try this method in a long-baked dessert like apple pie as the artificial sweetener loses its sweetening capacity at high temperatures over long periods. There are sweeteners that can be used in cooking and baking — saccharin (Sweet Magic®, Sweet 'N Low®, Sugar Twin®) and acesulfame-K (Sweet One™ and Swiss Sweet™). You cannot totally substitute artificial sweeteners for sugar in cakes or sweet breads, because the sugar provides bulk as well as sweetness to these recipes. Instead, try using a combination of sugar and a substitute. Cut the amount of sugar by 1/3 or 1/2, then replace the remaining sugar with artificial sweetener.

HOW TO SUBSTITUTE SWEETENERS FOR SUGAR

SUGAR	EQUAL OR SWEETMATE	SWEET 'N LOW	SWEET ONE OR SWISS SWEET*
2 tsp.	1 packet	1/5 tsp.	1 packet
1 Tbsp.	1 1/2 packets	1/3 tsp.	1 1/4 packets
1/4 c.	6 packets	3 packets	3 packets
1/3 c.	8 packets	4 packets	4 packets
1/2 c.	12 packets	6 packets (1 Tbsp.)	6 packets
2/3 c.	16 packets	8 packets	8 packets
3/4 c.	18 packets	9 packets (1 1/2 Tbsp.)	9 packets
1 c.	24 packets	12 packets (2 Tbsp.)	12 packets

* For best results, substitute half the sugar called for with the equivalent amount of Sweet One™ or Swiss Sweet™.

FAST FOOD RESTAURANTS

GUIDELINES FOR FAST FOODS

As well as using the equivalents list to convert your meal into bread, meat, and fat choices, there are other guidelines to follow in choosing items from fast-food menus.

1. Look out for hidden fats, especially if weight is a concern. Deep fat frying and batter coating can double or triple the number of calories.

2. Many food items contain ingredients from more than one food group. Fat is often a second ingredient. Portion sizes may need to be reduced in order to fit some of these food items into your meal plan.

3. Menu items such as pie, milkshakes, regular sodas, and even juices contain simple sugars. These items cannot be used in your meal plan.

4. Because of high fat and sodium content, fast foods should be used only occasionally.

McDONALD'S®

	FRUIT	BREAD	MEAT	FAT	VEG.	CAL.
+ Apple bran muffin	1	2	0	0	0	190
Egg McMuffin	0	2	2	1	0	290
+ English muffin (unbuttered)	0	2	0	0	0	160
Sausage (pork)	0	0	1	2	0	180
Scrambled eggs	0	0	2	0	0	140
Hashbrown potatoes	0	1	0	1	0	130
Big Mac	0	2 1/2	3	5	0	560
Cheeseburger	0	2	1	1 1/2	0	310
+ Hamburger	0	2	1	1/2	0	260
Quarter Pounder	0	2	2 1/2	1 1/2	0	410
Quarter Pounder with cheese	0	2	3	3	1	520
Filet-O-Fish	0	2 1/2	1	4	0	440
Small french fries	0	1 1/2	0	2	0	220
Chicken McNuggets (6 pieces)	0	1	2	1	0	290
McD.L.T.	0	2 1/2	2	3	0	580
+ McLean with Cheese	0	2	2	0	1	370
+ McLean without Cheese	0	2	2 1/2	0	1	320

+ = Better choice.

McDONALD'S®

	FRUIT	BREAD	MEAT	FAT	VEG.	CAL.
+ Chunky Chicken Salad	0	0	3	0	1	140
+ Grilled chicken sandwich with sauce (best to skip sauce)	0	2	2 1/2	0	0	415
McChicken	0	3 1/2	2	3 1/2	0	490
+ Garden Salad	0	0	1	0	1	110
Chef Salad	0	1/2	2 1/2	0	0	283

PIZZA HUT®

	FRUIT	BREAD	MEAT	FAT	VEG.	CAL.
Thin and Crispy Pizza (1 slice)						
+ Cheese	0	1	1 1/2	0	0	199
Pepperoni	0	1	1 1/2	1/2	0	206
Supreme	0	1 1/2	1 1/2	1/2	0	229
Thick and Chewy Pan Pizza (1 slice)						
+ Cheese	0	2	1	1	0	246
Pepperoni	0	2	1	2	0	270
Supreme	0	2	1	2	0	295

TACO BELL®

	FRUIT	BREAD	MEAT	FAT	VEG.	CAL.
Bean Burrito	0	3	1	2	0	343
Beef Burrito	0	2 1/2	3	2	0	466
+ Beef Tostada	0	1 1/2	2	1	0	291
+ Bellbeefer	0	1 1/2	2	1	0	221
+ Bellbeefer with Cheese	0	1 1/2	2	1	0	278
Burrito Supreme	0	3	2	3	0	457
Combination Burrito	0	3	2	2	0	404
Enchirito	0	3	3	2	0	454
+ Pintos n' Cheese	0	1 1/2	1	1/2	0	163
+ Tostado	0	1 1/2	1	1/2	0	179
+ Taco	0	1	2	0	0	186

+ = Better choice.

FAST FOOD RESTAURANTS

D'ANGELO®	FRUIT	BREAD	MEAT	FAT	VEG.	CAL.
+ Turkey D'Lite						
Pocket	0	2	3	0	1	350
Small Sub	0	2 1/2	3	0	1	390
+ Roast Beef D'Lite						
Pocket	0	2	3	0	1	325
Small Sub	0	2 1/2	3	0	1	365
+ Steak D'Lite						
Steak Pocket	0	2 1/2	4	0	1	415
Steak & Pepper Pocket	0	2 1/2	4	0	1	420
Steak & Mushroom Pocket	0	2 1/2	4	0	1	420
+ Chicken Stir Fry						
D'Lite Pocket	0	2	4	0	1	395
+ Vegetarian D'Lite						
Pocket	0	2 1/2	1	1 1/2	2	365
+ Super Salads:						
Turkey	0	2	3	0	2	375
Beef	0	2	2	0	2	350
Tuna	0	2	2	0	2	305
Chicken	0	2	3	0	2	380

WENDY'S®	FRUIT	BREAD	MEAT	FAT	VEG.	CAL.
+ Single Hamburger, plain	0	2	3	0	0	340
+ Single Hamburger, with everything	0	2	3	1	1	420
Wendy's® Big Classic	0	3	3	3	0	570
Jr. Hamburger	0	2	2	0	0	260
+ Jr. Cheeseburger	0	2	2	0	0	310
Jr. Bacon Cheeseburger	0	2	2	2	0	430
+ Jr. Swiss Deluxe	0	2	2	1	0	360
+ Kids Meal Hamburger	0	2	2	0	0	260
+ Kids Meal Cheeseburger	0	2	2	0	0	300
+ Grilled Chicken Sandwich	0	2	3	1	1	340

+ = Better choice.

WENDY'S®

	FRUIT	BREAD	MEAT	FAT	VEG.	CAL.
Chicken Sandwich	0	2 1/2	3	2	0	430
Chicken Club Sandwich	0	3	3	3	0	506
Fish Fillet Sandwich	0	3	2	3	0	460
+ Chili (regular) 9 oz.	0	1 1/2	2	0	0	220
+ Plain baked potato	0	3 1/2	0	0	0	270
+ Stuffed baked potatoes						
Broccoli with Cheese	0	3 1/2	1	2	0	400
Cheese	0	3 1/2	1	2	0	420
Chili and Cheese	0	4	2	2	0	500
Prepared Salads						
+ Chef	0	0	2	0	1	180
+ Garden	0	0	1	0	1	102
Taco	0	2 1/2	3	4	1	660
Salad Bar: free items in amount indicated:						
+ Alfalfa Sprouts (2 Tbsp.)						20
Bacon Bits (1 tsp.)						10
+ Croutons (10 pieces)						15
Egg (1 Tbsp.)						14
Other Items:						
Cheese (1 oz.)	0	0	1	0	0	90
Chow Mein Noodles (1/4 c.)	0	1/2	0	1/2	0	60
Cole Slaw (1/2 c.)	0	1/2	0	2	0	90
+ Breadstick (1)	0	1/2	0	0	0	20
+ Cottage Cheese (1/2 c.)	0	0	2	0	0	110
+ Green Peas (1/2 c.)	0	1	0	0	0	60
Pasta Salad (1/2 c.)	0	1	0	2	0	187
+ Turkey Ham (1/4 c.)	0	0	1	0	0	46
Salad Dressing (1 Tbsp.)						
Bleu Cheese	0	0	0	1 1/2	0	60
Celery Seed	0	0	0	1	0	70
Golden Italian	0	0	0	1 1/2	0	70
Oil	0	0	0	3	0	130

+ = Better choice.

FAST FOOD RESTAURANTS

WENDY'S®

	FRUIT	BREAD	MEAT	FAT	VEG.	CAL.
Ranch	0	0	0	2	0	80
Red French	0	1/2	0	1	0	70
1000 Island	0	0	0	1 1/2	0	70
+ Wine Vinegar	0	0	0	0	0	free
Low-Cal Bacon & Tomato	0	0	0	1	0	40
+ Low-Cal Creamy Cucumber	0	0	0	1	0	50
+ Low-Cal Italian	0	0	0	1/2	0	25
+ Low-Cal 1000 Island	0	0	0	1	0	40

BURGER KING®

	FRUIT	BREAD	MEAT	FAT	VEG.	CAL.
Whopper	0	3	3	4	0	670
Whopper with Cheese	0	3 1/2	4	6	0	760
Double Beef Whopper	0	3 1/2	5	6	0	890
Double Beef Whopper with cheese	0	3 1/2	6	7	0	980
Whopper Junior	0	2	2	2	0	370
Whopper Jr. w/Cheese	0	2	2	3	0	410
+ Hamburger	0	2	2	1	0	310
Cheeseburger	0	2	2	2	0	360
Double Cheeseburger	0	2	2	2	0	520
Chicken Sandwich	0	3	3	6 1/2	0	690
+ BK Broiler (without sauce)	0	2	3	0	0	300
Ham and Cheese	0	2 1/2	3	5	0	550
Veal Parmigiana	0	3	4	3	0	580
Whaler Sandwich	0	4	2	3 1/2	0	540
Whaler w/Cheese	0	4	2 1/2	4	0	590
French Fries (reg. order)	0	1 1/2	0	2	0	210
Onion Ring (reg. order)	0	2	0	3	0	270

+ = Better choice.

CHRONIMED PUBLISHING
BOOKS OF RELATED INTEREST

The Joslin Diabetes Self-Manager Series—All 6 Booklets
Booklets   004617 $17.70

Good Health with Diabetes...Through Exercise Joy Kistler, M.S., C.D.E., and Julie Rafferty. This informative, motivational booklet shows how to get started on an exercise program that's right for you, what pitfalls to watch out for, and how to integrate medication and food requirements with exercise.
Booklet   28 pages   004611 $29.50 (10 pack)

Eating Well, Living Better Joan Hill, R.D., C.D.E., Julie Goodwin, P.A., C.D.E., and Beverly Halford, R.D., C.D.E. Going beyond the basics of nutrition, this pamphlet addresses such issues as dining out, adjusting favorite recipes, and calculating exchanges, and others.
Booklet   32 pages   004612 $29.50 (10 pack)

Menu Planning— Simple! Joan Hill, R.D., C.D.E., Julie Goodwin, P.A., C.D.E., and Beverly Halford, R.D., C.D.E. Joslin's nutrition experts offer their clear and concise advice for understanding and using a meal plan to make eating delicious and enjoyable.
Booklet   32 pages   004613 $29.50 (10 pack)

Fighting Long-term Complications Richard S. Beaser, M.D., and Hugo Hollerorth, Ed.D. It's a fact of life with diabetes — the threat of eye, kidney, foot, nerve, cardiovascular, and other problems is always there. This booklet offers expert advise on how you can work with your health care team to minimize and treat these complications if they occur.
Booklet   32 pages   004614 $29.50 (10 pack)

The Foot Book Goeffery M. Habershaw, D.P.M., and Hugo Hollerorth, Ed.D. Here's an in-depth discussion of how diabetes can lead to foot problems, plus detailed information on how to avoid complications and treat them if they develop.
Booklet   32 pages   004615 $29.50 (10 pack)

Weight Loss—A Winning Battle Joan Hill, R.D., C.D.E., Julie Goodwin, P.A., C.D.E., and Beverly Halford, R.D., C.D.E. For many people with diabetes, taking pounds off — and keeping them off — is the key to better health. This motivational unit tells people with diabetes how and why to succeed.
Booklet   32 pages   004616 $29.95 (10 pack)

When Diabetes Complicates Your Life by Joseph Juliano, M.D. Dr. Juliano, an endocrinologist and research scientist, has had diabetes for 29 years and is now totally blind. He knows firsthand what it's like to combat the effects of diabetes. Empowering readers to find the motivation and information to control diabetes, Dr. Juliano shows how to avoid complications and overcome them if they occur.
004207   ISBN 1-56561-012-1 $9.95

Diabetes: A Guide to Living Well by Ernest Lowe and Gary Arsham, M.D., Ph.D. This comprehensive and up-to-date guide helps the person with diabetes design a program of individualized self-care and gain the willingness to follow it. It also tells how to deal with diet, exercise, stress, emotions, negative beliefs, and self-image.
004208   ISBN 1-56561-009-1 $12.95

It's Time to Learn about Diabetes by Jean Betschart, M.N., R.N., C.D.E. From fun exercises to family vacations, *It's Time to Learn About Diabetes* has everything school-age kids need to know about diabetes. It's a delightful, entertaining, and easy-to-use workbook that not only teaches children about what's happening to their bodies, but also helps them take care of themselves. Jean Betschart is president of the American Association of Diabetes Educators and coauthor of *Children with Diabetes*.
004084   ISBN 0-937721-80-8 $9.95

A Touch of Diabetes by Lois Jovanovic-Peterson, M.D., Charles M. Peterson, M.D., and Morton Stone. Everything people with newly diagnosed noninsulin-dependent diabetes need to know, from curbing potential complications to counting calories, is in this authoritative and easy-to-understand guide. Written by two of the foremost authorities on diabetes–Dr. Lois Jovanovic-Peterson and Dr. Charles M. Peterson–and the editor of *Diabetes in the News* magazine, Morton Stone, this book clearly shows how to control diabetes and improve quality of life.
004092   ISBN 0-937721-89-1 $7.95

When a Family gets Diabetes by Marge Heegaard, M.A., A.T.R., and Chris Ternand, M.D. This unique book uses art therapy to help children with diabetes and their families understand and verbally express their feelings about diabetes, themselves, and others. Here they draw pictures that relate to certain aspects of diabetes and discuss why they drew what they did.
004067   ISBN 0-937721-75-1 $6.95

Diabetes 101: A Pure and Simple Guide for People who Use Insulin by Richard O. Dolinar, M.D., and Betty Page Brackenridge, M.S., R.D., C.D.E. Here's a clear and easy-to-understand guide to the basic information needed by people using insulin to control diabetes, especially those newly diagnosed.
004065   ISBN 0-937721-63-8 $7.95

Diabetes Care Made Easy by Allison Nemaniec, R.N., Gretchen Kauth, R.D., and Marion Franz, R.D., M.S. Illustrated by Jan Westberg. Written and designed for both children and adults with limited reading skills, this breezy and easy-to-read book explains how to exercise and eat for better health, prevent foot problems, test blood sugar, cope with emotions, take insulin, and more.
004210   ISBN 1-56561-013-X $9.95

Diabetes: Actively Staying Healthy by Marion Franz, M.S., R.D., C.D.E., and Jane Norstrom, M.A. This is an essential and complete reference guide for diabetes and exercise. Highly motivational and with the latest facts, it has everything you need to know to participate safely at all levels of physical activity.
004056   ISBN 0-937721-57-3 $9.95

Learning to Live Well With Diabetes by Marion Franz, R.D., M.S., C.D.E., Donnell D. Etzwiler, M.D., Judy Ostrom Joynes, M.A., R.M., C.D.E., and Priscilla M. Hollander, M.D., Ph.D. You won't find a more comprehensive, authoritative, and easy-to-understand guide on managing diabetes than *Learning to Live Well With Diabetes*. Written by more than 25 prominent diabetes experts, this revised and updated edition reflects the latest medical advances, technologies, and research. In straightforward language, it explains how to take charge of your diabetes and live an active, healthy life. Plus, it contains over 200 useful illustrations, charts, and tables.
004083   ISBN 0-937721-79-4 $24.95

Managing Type II Diabetes by Arlene Monk, R.D., C.D.E., et al. Here's a basic guide for those who want to control Type II, or noninsulin-dependent, diabetes–rather than have it control them. Written by a team of diabetes specialists, this down-to-earth manual clearly explains what Type II diabetes is and how to manage it.
004022   ISBN 0-937721-24-7 $9.95

The Physician Within by Catherine Feste. Here internationally renowned health motivation specialist, Cathy Feste, focuses on motivating those with a health challenge, and anyone else, to stay on their regimen and follow healthy behavior.
004019   ISBN 0-937721-19-0 $8.95

Let Them Eat Cake by Virginia N. White with Rosa A. Mo., R.D. If you're looking for delicious and healthy pies, cookies, puddings, and cakes, this book will give you your just desserts. With easy, step-by-step instructions, this innovative cookbook features complete nutrition information, the latest exchange values, and tips on making your favorite snacks more healthful.
004206   ISBN 1-56561-011-3 $12.95

All-American Low-Fat Meals in Minutes by M.J. Smith R.D., L.D., M.A. Filled with tantalizing recipes and valuable tips, this cookbook makes great-tasting low-fat foods a snap for holidays, special occasions, or everyday. Most recipes take only minutes to prepare.
004079   ISBN 0-937721-73-5 $12.95

Convenience Food Facts by Marion Franz, R.D., M.S. and Arlene Monk, R.D., C.D.E. Includes complete nutrition information, tips, and exchange values on more than 1,500 popular name-brand processed foods commonly found in grocery store freezers and shelves. Helps you plan easy-to-prepare, nutritious meals.
004081   ISBN 0-937721-77-8 $10.95

Fast Food Facts by Marion Franz, R.D., M.S. This revised and up-to-date best-seller shows how to make smart nutrition choices at fast food restaurants–and tells what to avoid. Includes complete nutrition information on more than 1,000 menu offerings from the 21 largest fast food chains.
Standard-size edition   004068   ISBN 0-937721-67-0 $6.95
Pocket edition   004073   ISBN 0-937721-69-7 $4.95

Exchanges for All Occasions by Marion Franz, R.D., M.S. Exchanges and meal planning suggestions for just about any occasion, sample meal plans, special tips for people with diabetes, and more.
004201   ISBN 1-56561-005-9 $12.95

Buy them at your local bookstore or use this convenient coupon for ordering.

Order by mail:

CHRONIMED PHARMACY
P.O. Box 47945
Minneapolis, MN 55447-9727

Or order by phone:

1-800-848-2793
1-800-444-5951 *(non-metro area of Minnesota)*
612-546-1146 *(Minneapolis/St. Paul metro area)*
Please have your credit card number ready.

Please send me the books I have checked above. I am enclosing $_____. (Please add $3.00 to this order to cover postage and handling. Minnesota residents add 6.5% sales tax.) Send check or money order, no cash or C.O.D.'s. Prices are subject to change without notice.

Name _____

Address _____

City _____ State _____ Zip _____

Allow 4 to 6 weeks for delivery.
Quantity discounts available upon request.